Lord, Change Him
or Kill Him
and right now, I don't care which

Martha Rodriguez

Published by: Martha Rodriguez
supervised by
Scotchwood Hill Publishing Service
3101 Scotchwood Drive
Jonesboro, Arkansas 72405

ISBN: 979-8-9856361-4-7

Dedication

To those who have suffered as the fictional characters in this story—I have never walked in your shoes, but I pray for you.

Acknowledgment

I cannot imagine doing this work without the help of my friends and encouragers. My Beta readers, Beth Beck and Brenda Rawls let me know if something I've written isn't realistic. Debbie Archer shows me how to make my story stronger and better, and Pat Blake guides me as she patiently edits my messes and helps me fix what's wrong. I love these ladies and don't know what I'd do without them.

ONE

A slap sounded through the large kitchen and into the living room. "How dare you talk to that man. I won't have my wife acting like a floozy."

Lillian's hand went to her stinging face, and her jaw tensed. She would not cry. She would not give him the satisfaction. Thomas grabbed her by the throat and shoved her against the refrigerator. The strong smell of Mahogany Teakwood Cologne almost stifled her as she pulled at his fingers, trying to breathe. Her heart pounded against her chest so loud surely, he could hear it. When she slipped and nearly fell, he pulled her up by the neck.

"You do this every time," he said. "You know it infuriates me. I think you do it on purpose."

"Do what, Thomas? I haven't done anything."

"I saw the way you and Melvin looked at each other. It's obvious something's going on between you."

"He spoke to me, and I didn't want to be rude." She didn't understand why she had to defend herself for being friendly. "Why do you get so mad when someone speaks to me?"

"Your look said more than just hi. Are you seeing him while I'm at work?" His grip tightened, and her eyes bulged.

She sucked in a ragged breath. "No! Thomas, stop." She pulled at his hands. "I c-c-can't breathe."

He loosened his hold and shoved her. "You'd better not be." She fell to the floor, gasping. He pushed his pointed boot against her side, then kicked her. She gasped and doubled up as he stomped out the back door. She heard his truck back out of the garage and start down the drive.

She lay on the tile floor, rubbing her side. Now that he left, she could allow the tears to flow. She craned her neck to see what damage he had done. New red bruises would soon turn black, blue, then yellow like all the rest. If any appeared on her neck, he would insist she wear a turtleneck to cover them. In public, she maintained a cheerful front so people could not see her bruised spirit. Of course, he helped with that. He reminded her to hold her head up and smile when they were around other people. Of course.

She had few regrets until she married the dark, handsome county judge, Thomas Thorn, to the chagrin of most of the single ladies around town. When a car accident took the life of her sweet, gentle husband, Jim, she was devastated. Thomas charmed her with his compassion and assisted her when the insurance company challenged her insurance policy. He soon became a part of her everyday life, sharing her concerns until she was convinced that she needed him. Her grown twins, Eva and Brody, had families of their own. Eva taught third grade in the local elementary school, and Brody worked as a licensed electrician. Proud of them, she wished she could see them more often.

After she and Thomas married, he gradually became more possessive and controlling. At first, she made excuses for his behavior. When she realized his controlling behavior had consumed her, she tried to stand up for herself, and he became violent. He became so angry over the least little thing, he scared her. When she wanted to have her kids over or visit them, he had such a fit that she stopped mentioning it. She had to be satisfied to talk with them on the phone once a week after he went to work. If they had the faintest idea what was happening to her, they would come to rescue her.

But no, she wouldn't tell them. She had to live with her decision to marry Thomas — for better or worse. She would honor her vows because her nature demanded it. She held herself to a high standard. Besides, she knew the Bible spoke against divorce. She never wanted to do anything to displease God.

Groaning, she picked herself up from the floor and entered the bathroom. A hot shower would soothe her aching body. Again, she allowed the tears but quickly wiped them away. By now, she should stop crying, but crying helped when she cried out to God. At least, she thought it did. But why wouldn't He help her get out of this mess? Maybe if she had asked for wisdom about marrying Thomas, He would have stopped her. Maybe He tried to warn her, but she wouldn't listen. No matter. She had no doubts that her heavenly Father loved her and would help her. He always had.

Jim talked often about the love of God. "God loves us endlessly," he would say. "His love is incomprehensible. It is unconditional." That love provided her with joy and peace, first through Jim's love and then through her own relationship with God. But lately, she had begun to think she wasn't worthy of anyone's love, much less God's.

She brushed her shoulder-length salt and pepper hair, pushed it behind her ears, spritzed on some Channel 5, and applied makeup to her slender face and almond-shaped hazel eyes before entering the kitchen. She began gathering the dirty dishes from the table and lit a candle to eliminate the smell of fried eggs, bacon, and toast, Thomas' everyday breakfast. She didn't dislike the smell of bacon and eggs. Rather, the day-in, day-out smell permeated the house and infused her brain with the monotony that had become her life since she had married this man.

Jim loved a variety of breakfast foods, much the same as he loved the diversity in everything about life. He loved the challenge of change and trying different things. They always ate together before they drove off to work — he to the post office and she to her customer service job at a large department store. Under the pretense of wanting her to be a lady of leisure, Thomas had insisted she quit her job and stay home. Now she understood the reason. If she were home all the time, she couldn't see her friends, and he could control her every move.

She swallowed the last of her cup of coffee and looked at the duty list he left for her. Humpf! As if she'd never cleaned house before. Clean the kitchen, it read. Vacuum the rug. Dust every room. Clean and disinfect the bathroom. Wash the sheets. Iron my pants. Wash the windows. Sweep the moon. Arrange the stars. Mop the planet Mars. She jerked the list from the refrigerator and threw it on the counter. Ugh! For the first time in her life, she hated housework. She loved keeping the house when her Jim lived. They worked together, and she hummed as she mopped and dusted while he vacuumed and did laundry. She shuddered as she looked at the clock and picked up a dishrag. She'd better get started. She regretted selling the house she and Jim shared, but Thomas insisted she sell it and move into his home. Yet he made it plain from the beginning that it was *his* house. He fussed at her when she moved a piece of furniture to accommodate an heirloom table that she brought with her. She couldn't change her mind about selling the house then. When he arrived home from his job at the city hall, Thomas would inspect the house. She gritted her teeth. Wonder how he would like it if she went to his office and inspected his work every day?

Stopping long enough to eat some cheese and crackers, she folded the last of the sheets and shoved them into the linen closet. She glanced at the clock. Two ten. Good. After she went to the barn to check on the cows and goats, she would have time to watch Reba reruns before getting dinner ready. Monday, pork chops. Tuesday, meatloaf. Wednesday, fried potatoes, fried cornbread that he liked to call johnnycakes, ham, and beans; Thursday, fried chicken; and Friday, fish. On Saturdays, he usually asked for a sandwich, and on Sundays, she rose early to prepare smothered steak or pot roast with mashed potatoes before church and heated corn and browned hot rolls when they arrived home later. She may as well learn to live with a creature of habit.

TWO

Kora smiled as Nathan surrounded her with his strong arms and pulled her to his chest. Next week, they would celebrate their second anniversary, and he said he would take her to a movie after dinner at a nice restaurant. His brown eyes sparkled as he pushed her blonde hair back from her face and kissed her, first on the forehead, then the nose, and down to the chin.

"My beautiful blue-eyed bride," he said. "I love you so much. I'm so glad you said yes when I asked you to marry me."

"I'm glad you asked." Her heart rate quickened as she returned the kiss. She had no idea anyone could love her like this. Her dad had been against the marriage from the start, but she ignored his negative opinion of Nathan. She hoped her dad would learn to like his son-in-law, although, in two years, he still scowled every time he saw them.

"Every time we visit your family," Nathan once said with a shudder, "your dad looks at me like he would enjoy nothing better than to kill me or at least sell me to some cannibals somewhere."

She reached up to touch his sandy-colored hair over his ear. "Looks like you need a haircut," she said. "But not too soon. I like it a little long." She started to pull away, but he held on. "I have to finish dinner," she said. "It's almost done."

"What are you making? I'm hungry."

"I thought I had a tomato to make tacos, but I guess I didn't pick one up at the store. I forgot to add them to my list. I've been so busy lately. I had a little trouble meeting a deadline at work. I did get some chicken the other day, so I'm making chicken strips."

Nathan frowned, and his eyes darkened. "Again? Didn't we have those two days ago?"

"Yes. I'm sorry. Those are easy, and I'm really tired." She sighed. "My boss wanted me to work over, but I wiggled out of it. Derick said he would fill in for me."

His frown deepened. "Who's Derick? Is he new?"

She sprinkled salt and black pepper on the chicken and dipped it in a mixture of eggs and milk. "He started about a month ago, so he's not real new. We have another one who started last week. He's a fast learner, so he'll likely do well. Mr. Moore seems to like him."

He paced as she rolled the chicken in a flour mixture and added it to the hot oil. "How about you? Do you like him?"

She stopped in the middle of chopping vegetables for a salad and looked at him. His tone sounded different. Something was off. "Yes, he's nice. So far, I see nothing to make me dislike him."

He pulled plates from the cabinet and set the table, slamming the plates and silver so hard they clinked and rattled.

Kora's eyes widened. "Is something wrong? Be careful. Those plates are breakable."

He whirled, fury in his eyes. "I think I know how to set the table. I've done it enough times in the last two years." He grabbed two glasses and filled them with ice and sweet tea. "I don't like you working with those men," he muttered.

"What?" She pulled out Italian dressing from the refrigerator. "They're my co-workers, Nathan. I don't understand what the problem is."

He moved across the room in three steps and gripped her arm. When she winced, he loosened his grip and embraced her. His eyes were still angry, but his tone now gentle.

"You're my wife, and I won't stand anyone—I mean anyone—even looking at you. You hear?"

She swallowed hard and turned her face away from him. He put a finger under her chin and pulled her face back around. Then he kissed her long and hard until she gasped and pulled back. She touched her bruised lips.

"What's wrong with you?" she said. Then she snickered. "Nathan, are you jealous? I think you are." She put a hand on his chest and gave him a little shove. "You'll never have a reason to be jealous of me, sweetheart. I'm all yours, now and forever."

His face brightened, and his lips moved over her hair and face until he reached her lips. A tender and loving kiss quickened her heartbeat.

"Now, that's my Nathan," she said. "The love of my life. The sweet man I married." She planted another kiss on his lips and turned to check on the strips. He turned on the television and slumped in his recliner. He remained quiet through the meal and at bedtime, speaking only to answer her when she spoke.

Every day for the next two weeks, his mood fluctuated between sweet, loving, and attentive to distant, contemptuous, and angry. When she wanted to visit her family, he refused.

"Okay," she said. "If you don't want to go, I'll go alone. I haven't seen them in over a month."

His face darkened. "No, you won't."

She couldn't believe it. "I can't go see my family? Why? You see your family when you want to."

He jerked his hand up, then dropped it. "Kora, you're a

grown woman. You don't have to see your mama all the time. So just forget it. You're not going."

Stunned, she put her hands to her cheeks and ran into the bedroom. Had he intended to hit her? No, surely not. He wouldn't do that. But lately, he seemed so different. So angry. His demeanor scared her. She considered going over his objections but decided it wouldn't be worth the fight. She would go later. She needed to see her mama once in a while.

Three days later, Nathan came home with a big smile, grabbed her, and whirled her around. "I did it, sweetie. I got that promotion. Now I earn enough for you to stay home. Aren't you excited? You don't have to work anymore."

"What are you talking about?" She stepped back from him. "I'm proud of you, Nathan. You've worked hard for that promotion. But I want to work. I love my job and have worked hard to get where I am."

"No!" He exploded. "You're getting outta that place, Kora. Today!"

She cowered and bit her lip. "I—I don't understand. Why are you demanding I quit my job? What's wrong?"

He grabbed her arm and jerked her close, his eyes boring into hers. He spoke through clenched teeth. "I said you're quitting, and that's what I mean. Got it?" He shoved her away and walked out the back door.

She sat on the edge of an armchair and covered her face with shaking hands. Sobs racked her body. How could he do this to her? What happened to her sweet Nathan? How had he turned into a monster in such a short time? When the back door opened, she ran into the bathroom and locked the door.

"Kora? Where are you, sweetheart?"

That sounded more like the voice of her sweet Nathan, but she couldn't face him yet. She sat on the toilet and tried to calm herself. Her chest rose and fell, and trembling hands wiped her wet face.

"Kora? Come on, sweetie. I'm sorry I had to get rough. I want what's best for you. And me. For us. Don't you understand?"

No, she didn't understand. The sweet, loving man she married two short years ago was now acting like a control freak. She recalled a few times before they were married when a hint of jealousy had popped up, but just for a moment. She assumed any jealous feelings would disappear after they married. He never hid the fact that he didn't like her family, but he always allowed her to visit them. And he congratulated her when she landed a coveted job with Shelton Enterprises.

Then she remembered how he acted when he met her boss. Mr. Dewey did look quite handsome with his black hair and mustache, but Kora didn't pay attention until Nathan made a remark about him. Nathan refused to smile at the man and barely acknowledged him when she introduced them. She brushed off her embarrassment when Nathan smothered her with apologies and kisses afterward.

"Mr. Dewey is happily married, and so am I," she said. "I have no interest in him except as my boss. You have no worries about me. I'm faithful 'til death."

As she thought about it, other things popped into her head. Once, as they were driving home from town, he scolded her about talking a mite too long to a man in the line at the DMV. She didn't think much of it, but after that, she carefully avoided conversations with people she didn't know, especially men. Another time, they met one of her co-workers in the grocery store, and Nathan's eyes snapped when she responded to his greeting. She spent the rest of the day trying to convince him the man meant nothing to her. She hadn't thought much about that either, until now. What was going on with her husband? She didn't know, and she sure didn't like it.

THREE

*B*ella slapped peanut butter and strawberry jelly on a piece of bread, stuck it in a paper bag with a box of apple juice, and handed it to fifteen-year-old Trevor. "Have a good day at school, son," she said as she pecked him on the cheek.

"Thanks, Mom." He turned. "Come on, Addie. The bus is coming." Thirteen-year-old Addison grabbed her lunch bag and hugged Bella.

"Later, Mom," she yelled as she ran out the door.

Bella put away the peanut butter and jelly and wiped the counter. She took such pride in their new home, having moved from an old, rundown farmhouse to the new two-story brick home just down the road. Levi had been ecstatic when the people who built the house put it up for sale a year later.

"They lived in it just long enough to break it in," he said with a huge grin behind his shaggy red beard.

The house nestled under a grove of oak trees with a large pond nearby. When the kids begged for a canoe and jet skis for the pond, Levi told them they could clean the barn stalls and care for the livestock to earn extra money. They tackled the job with gusto the first few weeks, but before long, they lagged in completing their chores.

She threw a load of jeans into the washing machine, put on her boots, and headed for the barn. She worked two days a week at the hospital doing office work. On her days off, she enjoyed working outside with the herd of cattle and the few goats Levi had purchased within the last couple of years. She fed them corn and pampered them with sliced apples and carrots. Levi laughed at her when she gave each animal a name.

"You shouldn't make pets of them," he said. "You'll be sad when I sell them. I don't want to see you sad."

Yeah, right. He really hated to see her sad. Humph! She picked up a pitchfork and stabbed it into a stack of hay. She jerked off a chunk and threw it over into the stall. Her favorite cow, Bessie, would love her for the nice bedding. What would it take to get the crankiness out of her man? Levi could be so loving and kind, then turn around and snap her head off.

She hated it when he yelled at her for the most minor things. Like last night. He didn't like the way she fried his bologna. "You burned it," he complained. So, she cooked it just a little browner than he liked. And that happened only because she was removing the thick mud from his pants legs before she threw them into the washer and was sidetracked. He really hit the ceiling when she forgot to pick up a pack of cigarettes for him. She thought he would smack her. He had never laid a hand on her, but he had come close. He may as well, though, because his tone hit her like a brickbat. The old saying, 'sticks and stones may break your bones, but words will never hurt you,' was a myth. Experience had taught her that internal bruises left by angry, hateful words take much longer to heal than external ones. The wounds deep inside her kept layering one on top of another until they affected every aspect of her life.

She stabbed another fork of hay and threw it into the stall. He didn't need cigarettes anyway. He said he would quit smoking, but she didn't see that happening. Her own health and the health of the kids concerned her. She'd read that secondhand smoke caused more damage than firsthand smoke. When she told him that, he laughed and blew cigarette smoke in her face. Didn't he even care that she and the kids were affected by his crude behavior and his bad habits? Just because he was raised in a dysfunctional home didn't excuse him for causing their home to be that way. Stab. Jab. Toss. Hay flew into the air. She removed her hair clip and ran her fingers through her long auburn hair to remove pieces of straw.

They did have some good times together, though. She loved the times they loaded the kids and some luggage into the car and took a short vacation to fun places, mostly rivers and lakes. They set up an old tent they'd had for years, and she cooked the fish that Levi and the kids caught. Levi taught the kids to swim and fish, and he laughed at her when she described the huge, horrible creatures she imagined living under the water. Once, he talked her into riding a tube behind a speedboat in the lake. She did well until they met another boat, and she held on for dear life while the tube bounced over the large waves. Then he turned the boat and flung her off the tube. She floundered in the water until he circled around to pick her up. Trevor and Addie thought that the trick was hilarious.

She had to laugh when she remembered them trying to doctor a sick cow. The veterinarian gave them needles and medicine and told them to give her a shot once a day for three days. They ran into trouble when they couldn't pierce the cow's thick skin with the needle. Bella held her head to keep her still while Levi tried to insert the needle, but the cow's huge body heaved, and she pulled away from Bella. The needle bent when Levi tried to stick it in. Of course, the real problem lay in their lack of knowledge about the chore.

"Let me try it," Bella said, so he handed her another needle. When she tried to administer the shot, the cow moved away. She looked around for Levi. He stood outside the barn door, peeping in.

"What are you doing out there?" Bella yelled. "You're supposed to be in here holding the cow." She jabbed the needle hard, and it finally pierced the skin. She did the job without the help of her brave husband.

She loved that grouch. They had been so happy the first years of their marriage, and she believed they could be happy again. She prayed. "Lord, please change my man. I want my children to have a good father. One they can go to with their problems. One who will listen to them. One who will take them to church and be an example of Your love. One who will attend their activities and cheer for them, even if they don't win. I want a loving husband, a man of integrity, who will listen to and support me. One like John Walton or Charles Ingles."

She admired these father/husband characters on television shows she enjoyed, *The Waltons* and *Little House on the Prairie*.

"And Lord, will You please talk to him about attending church with us? Thanks."

FOUR

*L*illian looked at Thomas out of the corner of her eye as they drove to the church they attended regularly. She admired his liquid brown eyes and thought the small goatee he wore gave his chin prominence. She loved the dimples that appeared on his tanned face when he smiled. Bits of gray at his temples gave him a distinguished look. So far this morning, he had been amiable, unlike the day before. His mood fluctuated so rapidly that she never suspected when something she said would backfire, causing her to suffer his fury. When they arrived, Pastor Bill and his wife, Katie, greeted them at the door.

"How's it going, friend?" Pastor Bill slapped Thomas on the shoulder and guided him to his office. "I have something to talk over with you," he said as he opened the door. Thomas followed him, and Katie smiled at Lillian.

"Your husband is so special," Katie said. "We think the world of him. We're so glad he started coming to church here. I think his attendance really did help him win the county judge election." She lowered her voice. "Bill wants him to be on the Service Outreach Committee. To serve on any committee, a person must have integrity and wisdom. We feel your Thomas is the one we need to help our church be more involved in local charitable causes. We think it's good for our church and for the community."

"Oh, sure. The church needs to be involved in local

crusades." Lillian forced a smile and tried to look happy. Her Thomas? Really? Well, maybe if he would focus on this assignment, he would be kinder to her. She nodded at Katie, who turned to other church members demanding her attention. Lillian greeted people as she went to her seat. She once had close friends in this group, but Thomas had stopped her Christian fellowship and every other kind of fellowship. Now, they nodded, smiled at her, and moved on to talk to someone else. Most likely, they considered her stuck up. One lady remarked that marrying an important man didn't make a woman better than other women. She wished she could talk with them like she had before Thomas.

During the service, the choir sang her favorite song, *The Goodness of God*. Tears stung her eyes as she thought about the lyrics. If He was so good, why didn't he change Thomas? She reminded herself that Thomas had free will and must choose to change. She sighed. Pastor Bill stood behind the pulpit and opened his Bible.

"Please turn to Colossians chapter three, starting with verse one," he said. A moment of rustling Bible pages sounded, and then he started to read. Lillian found the scriptures and followed along

"Set your minds on things above, not on earthly things." Guess she'd have to try that while Thomas berated her. "Rid yourself of all such things as these: anger, rage, malice, slander... do not lie to each other." She hoped Thomas listened. He lied to her yesterday when he lashed out at her for no reason and then said he loved her.

"Wives, submit yourselves to your husbands, as is fitting in the Lord." Pastor paused and looked over the congregation. Thomas put an arm around her shoulders and patted her, nodding his head. Pastor continued to read. "Husbands, love your wives, and do not be harsh with them."

As Pastor read, Thomas stiffened and flipped through his

Bible as though searching for something. He laid his Bible on the pew and leaned over to whisper to her.

"I have to go see to the offering plate. I'll be back later." Then he was gone. She was disappointed but not surprised. When Pastor Bill started a sermon about marriage or a Godly attitude, Thomas always left to count the offering plate or check to see if the children's church leaders needed something. In fact, anymore he seldom stayed to hear any sermon. She could expect him to use the scriptures to browbeat her when they were home later. That's what he always did.

"The Bible says wives submit to your husbands," he would yell if she tried to defend herself from his verbal abuse.

At the end of the service, Pastor Bill shook the hand Thomas extended. "My good man," he said, "you're a pillar of this church. I know I can always count on you."

When Lillian turned her head to hide her disgust, her eyes met with a new church member whose husband was ushering her out the door. The woman bit her lower lip and raised her eyebrows. Regretting her actions, Lillian blushed. She could only imagine what her expression had been. She turned to smile at Pastor Bill.

Thomas put an arm around her and squeezed. "Lillian and I are glad to serve where we're needed," he said. "Aren't we, dear?"

Lillian nodded but said nothing. He scowled to let her know her response didn't please him. She didn't see him allowing her to serve on any church committee, even though she would like nothing better. She knew he expected her to verbally agree with his comment and show support for anything he said. She would most likely hear his outrage on the way home. Oh well, it wouldn't be the first time. But one day, it would end. It had to. She couldn't take much more.

As they started toward their vehicle, someone yelled at them.

"Hey, Thomas. Lillian. Wait a minute." Brian and April Robins, a couple close to their age, walked toward them. "We want you to have lunch with us," Brian said. "April cooked a roast this morning, and we'd like to share it with you."

April laughed. "Yes, I think I cooked a little too much for the two of us. I made it with potatoes and carrots, and I have green beans and salad. More than plenty to share."

Lillian looked at Thomas, who frowned. "I'm sorry, but we must get right home," she said. "Maybe another time."

Thomas gripped her arm and laughed. "Why, Lillian, what are you talking about?" He turned to Brian and April. "Sure, we can go. We'd love to have lunch with you."

Heat moved from Lillian's neck to her face. Other people had asked them to lunch, and he scolded her when she wanted to accept the invitations. She wanted to choke him. Instead, she forced a smile and nodded.

When she crawled into the truck and closed the door, he smirked. "Why are you making excuses? It's my job to say whether we accept an invitation to lunch."

"I guess I didn't know that," she murmured. "What about the lunch I made this morning?"

"Well, next time, you'd better remember it." He jammed the truck into gear, looked back, and pulled onto the road. "We can eat it tomorrow. And you'd better behave today."

She gasped. "What do you think I'm going to do? Eat with my fingers? Wipe my mouth on my sleeve? Break my glass? Forget to say please and thank you?"

"Sometimes you talk too much," he said. "Sometimes you can be a bit too friendly."

"So," she looked at him sideways, "it's okay for you to be friendly, but not for me?"

He slapped the steering wheel. "You never mind about me," he yelled. "You just watch yourself."

Their hosts greeted them at the door. Lillian admired the

stylish home while Thomas and Brian talked about sports and politics. Lillian talked only when someone directed the conversation to her, staying quiet until the men went outside to look at an ATV. Then, she helped April clear the table.

"Are you always so quiet?" April asked. "Is something wrong? Maybe you and Thomas quarreled on the way over here? I can't imagine either one of you being disagreeable, but I guess everyone is at some time." She looked askance, and a one-sided smile flitted across her face.

Lillian picked up some plates. "I'm not feeling very well. That's all."

"I'm sorry. Is there something I can get you? Maybe you need to sit down. Did the food disagree with you?"

"No, I'm all right. I didn't sleep well last night. I'm just tired." Lillian searched her mind for something to say to lighten the mood. "I loved your fruit salad. Would you give me the recipe? Thomas liked it. Maybe I can make it for him."

April brightened. "Sure, I'll give it to you. It's easy to make." She grabbed a pen and paper and wrote it down. They spent the rest of the afternoon talking about cooking, recipes, and favorite meals.

When she and Thomas started home, he quizzed her. "What did you and April talk about?" he asked. He studied her face when she answered.

"Just cooking and recipes and stuff like that," she said. "Don't worry — I didn't tell her how mean you are to me."

"What? You think I'm mean to you?" His fingers tightened on the steering wheel so hard his knuckles turned white. "Woman, you haven't seen mean yet."

She cringed and dreaded going home. What would he do to her? When they arrived, a red sports car sat in their drive.

"Wonder what he's doing here." Thomas jumped out and threw his arms around the grinning red-headed man who stepped out of the car. He turned as Lillian closed the truck door. "Lillian, this is my cousin Will." He slapped the man on the back. "I haven't seen him in over a year."

Lillian smiled and nodded at the man, and when Thomas guided him onto the front porch, she fled into the house. She could only hope the visiting cousin would put Thomas in a good mood that would last a few days.

She put away the food she had cooked for lunch and went into the bedroom. A little notebook lay on the nightstand by the bed. She picked it up and flipped through the pages. She picked up a pen. When she wrote her thoughts and feelings in the journal, a sense of peace filled her heart.

Dear Journal: It has been quite a day. My husband is now the chairman of a church committee. I'm sure he'll do a good job. I am still nothing but a tiny speck in the scheme of things. Maybe someday I'll be promoted.

I used to be very involved in church activities. I helped with VBS in the summer and often taught a youth group. I always took special dishes to church dinners. I enjoyed that. Once, I even taught a ladies' bible study. I loved that.

Sometimes, those same ladies look at me as though I've turned into a slacker. I hope they don't think badly of me since I've married and stopped doing anything at church. I pray they don't think I've set myself up as too good to work. They can't know that I would help in a second if I could. I miss that life.

FIVE

*L*illian woke to the sound of music and the smell of coffee brewing. She stretched, yawned, and then jumped up. Thomas must have risen early to go to work. But wait. It's Saturday. He usually slept later on Saturdays.

She peeped into the kitchen to see him busy at the stove. She smelled bacon. He hadn't cooked anything in the few years they were married. She went into the bathroom to shower, all the while wondering what got into him.

When she finished her toiletries and entered the kitchen, breakfast sat on the table.

"There you are," he said. Dimples appeared when he smiled, and he embraced her before he pulled out her chair. He poured her a cup of coffee and sat across from her. He took her hand, blessed the food, and served her waffles, eggs, bacon, and coffee.

She accepted his attentions, her eyes wide. "You made breakfast for me?" She picked up her fork. "You've never done this before."

"Can't a man do something nice for his sweetheart?" He leaned over and kissed her cheek. "I cooked a lot before I married you. In fact, I pride myself on being a pretty good chef."

"Thank you," she whispered. She took a few bites. "This is wonderful. You can cook breakfast for me anytime."

"One day I'll make you some chicken marsala with salad, and I can make a mean garlic bread." Her heart rate quickened as his warm hand rested on her shoulder.

"That sounds wonderful," she said. "I didn't know you liked pasta. Or salad."

He winked at her. "Sure, I do. It isn't my favorite food, but I do like it."

When they finished the meal, he rose and picked up the dishes from the table.

"What are you doing?" she asked. "I'll clean up."

"Oh, no, my dear. I'll clean up the kitchen. You take the day off and relax. Read a book. Do something you like to do."

She stared at him. She had never seen this side of him before. Hopefully, it would last—like, forever. Could it be a dream from which she would awaken? She hoped not.

As he suggested, she spent much of the day reading, then went for a walk and finished the day sitting in a lounge chair in the backyard, watching the squirrels and birds. That evening, he pulled her into his lap, and they watched a romantic movie. He carried her to their bed and showed her his romantic side. It had been a while. They fell asleep snuggling together.

On Sunday morning, when the choir sang, tears overwhelmed Lillian. The special Saturday she had experienced the day before had ended. This morning, things were back to, "You can't do anything right!" with an unseemly eye-roll. When she failed to make his coffee strong enough to suit him, he berated her and made her feel like dirt. "Look at this mess. Anyone could do better than this," he said as he flicked crumbs from the kitchen counter. Her shoulders sagged, and her hands trembled as she stood and tried to focus on the words of the familiar song, "It Is Well." Could she actually say, 'It is well with my soul'? Thomas's moods, sweet one day, monster the next, made it worse. She heard his baritone voice as he sang the chorus, but she tensed as he slipped an arm around her shoulders and sang the lyrics.

When Pastor Bill stood behind the pulpit and opened his Bible, Lillian turned to 1 Peter. "Today I'm talking about Walking Daily with Christ," he said. Thomas slipped his arm around her again and pulled her toward him. He smiled when she glanced at him and patted her hand that lay on top of her Bible. As Pastor Bill spoke about how a Christian should behave, Thomas fidgeted. First, he lifted his arm from around Lillian. Then he grabbed her Bible and flipped through it. Finally, he laid the Bible onto her lap, leaned over, and whispered into her ear.

"I'm going to the office to take care of some things. Don't forget, we're going straight home after church, so don't be standing around gabbing."

Near the service's end, Lillian went to the bathroom. When she passed the office, Thomas sat with his feet up on the desk, his eyes closed. She entered the empty bathroom and leaned against the sink to look in the mirror. Did he treat her with disrespect because she no longer looked pretty and young? No, that couldn't be it, or he wouldn't have married her. Then what?

Tears stung her eyes, and she grabbed a tissue from the counter. She didn't usually cry much, but the hurt kept building day after day until she could feel her soul weakening. What could she do to remedy the situation? She shook her head when the word 'divorce' popped into her mind. That's funny. Divorce never entered the conversation between her and Jim, no matter how much they argued in their twenty-nine years together. Not that they didn't have troubles. They fought like any other couple. Some days, they didn't like each other, but they always loved each other. They never questioned that their place was together for better or worse, "till death do us part." They took their wedding vows seriously.

She blew her nose and threw the tissue into the trash as the door opened, and Kora Stormes walked in. Kora was new to the church, so Lillian had never talked to her. Lillian smiled at the younger woman.

"Are you all right?" Kora asked. "I'm sorry, but I thought you were crying."

Lillian took another tissue and wiped her eyes. "Allergies," she said. "You know — this time of year."

"Sure." Kora stepped into a stall, and Lillian started to leave when Kora spoke again. "Aren't you Thomas Thorn's wife? Is he okay? I saw him leave earlier. I'm sorry. I don't mean to be so nosey."

Lillian stepped away from the door and glanced into the mirror again. "Yes, Thomas is my husband. He's always busy during church."

"Oh." Pause. "Doesn't he like to hear Pastor Bill preach? I've noticed he seldom stays during the sermon."

"You're very observant," Lillian said. "Most people don't notice."

Kora flushed, left the stall, and washed her hands. "I guess I am, but we sit two rows behind you, so I see him leave. Again, I don't mean to be nosey."

Lillian looked at the young woman and suddenly burst into tears. She grabbed a tissue and sobbed into it.

"Oh." Kora touched her arm. "I'm so sorry. I—I didn't mean...."

"It—it isn't you," Lillian said. "It's just that I—I mean—I can't stand it anymore. I don't know what to do." For some unknown reason, the look in the eyes of this younger woman pulled at her heartstrings. She dabbed her eyes and tried to compose herself. "I'm sorry. I don't mean to bother you with my problems."

Kora's eyes glistened. "I never would have guessed you had any problems. You're always so confident and composed." Her sweet face held such compassion Lillian wanted to get to know her. "Would you like to talk about it?" Kora asked.

Lillian smiled. "I would, but I think the service is about over. I must hurry, or I'll be in trouble. Thomas doesn't like it when I stay to talk to people."

"Oh." Kora's face clouded. "But I see him talking to people."

"Yeah, well, that's him. It's okay for him, but not me."

"I understand. Nathan's kinda like that, too. Sometimes, he gets mad when he sees me talking to someone. He's getting worse about it. I don't understand him most of the time. He's like a bipolar cat."

Lillian laughed. "I think all cats are bipolar." She glanced at her watch. "I would like to talk to you. Do you think we could meet somewhere this week? I'd love to visit with you."

Kora's eyes lit up, and they agreed to meet at Kora's house for lunch on Wednesday. Lillian splashed water on her face, patted it dry, and hurried out to meet Thomas, who talked to one of the deacons. She stood beside him until he finished his conversation, nodding to those who spoke to her. She hoped her eyes weren't red, or he would scold her and ask questions about it. He took her arm, and no one could see the pressure he exerted as he squeezed it. She took care not to wince.

SIX

Kora opened the door and welcomed Lillian on Wednesday. In the spacious kitchen, she had spread a simple lunch of chicken salad, crackers, and lemon bars on her butcher block bar. Dressed in white capris and a floral top, Lillian looked fresh and comfortable. Kora hugged her and offered her a chair.

"I'm so happy you could come today," she said to the older woman. "I feared you wouldn't."

Lillian smiled. "I almost didn't. Thomas keeps track of what I do and gets mad if I go somewhere or someone comes to see me. But I figured out a way he won't know." She took a sip of sweet tea and bowed her head as Kora blessed the food. "This looks great," she said as she took a bite. "Ummm! It tastes great, too. I need your recipes."

"So—what did you do to keep him from knowing?"

"He only knows if he sees car tracks on the drive, so I walked. It isn't far, and I need to walk anyway."

"Wait—where do you live?"

"We live about a half mile off Highway 15."

Kora gasped. "It has to be at least three miles to my house from yours."

"More like three and a half." Lillian grinned. "Walking keeps me in shape and gives me alone time. I know I'm alone all day while Thomas is at work, but I love to get away from the house sometimes. It's like freedom." She frowned. "The house feels like a prison because I'm forced to stay there day in and day out."

"Why does your husband do that? I mean, why does he keep track of everything you do? You mean you don't go grocery shopping alone?"

"Oh, no, not alone. He goes with me when we go to town for anything. He's afraid I'll see someone and talk to them. He doesn't trust me."

Kora fiddled with her napkin. "Nathan accuses me of flirting if I even look at another male. He made me quit work. I hate the feeling. He makes me feel guilty of doing something wrong." She laid the napkin on the table. "I've been praying for him to start attending church with me. I think church would change him. But I don't know if I want him to. At least I can talk freely when I'm there without him."

"Does his family attend church?" Lillian asked.

"His mom does sometimes. She works a lot on weekends. His parents divorced when he was eight. His dad abused him and his mom, and after the divorce, Nathan saw little of him. You'd think Nathan wouldn't be abusive since he saw how it affected him and his mom. She's remarried now. Her present husband is a good guy."

"Seems like it, but often, an abused child grows up to become an abuser. That's sad."

"I never would have thought he'd turn out like this. He was always so sweet to me when we dated."

After two hours of sharing and chatting, Lillian hugged Kora and started home. She enjoyed the walk but kept thinking of how she could help her young friend. She didn't want to see

Nathan abuse Kora like Thomas did her. Since they were both young and newly married, surely the jealousy and manipulation could be stopped somehow. She hated to see Kora miserable in her marriage. She hadn't had a wonderful marriage to compare. Lillian wished every woman could have a wonderful relationship like she'd had with Jim.

When she arrived home, she finished a load of laundry, checked on the livestock, and started supper. The phone showed a missed call from a number she didn't recognize, and she deleted it. Probably a telemarketer. The beans in the crock were done, and the potatoes were frying when Thomas walked into the door.

"Where have you been today?" he demanded. "You didn't answer the phone."

"You called?" Lillian laid a spoon on the counter.

"I didn't, but the insurance agent did. He said no one answered."

"I must have been outside," she said. "I went to check on the stock and had to fill the water tank again. It's hot, so they are drinking a lot. I saw a missed call but didn't recognize it, so I deleted it." She needed a distraction. "Looks like Bootsey will deliver any day now. She sure is big. I'm bettin' she'll have twins. Maybe triplets."

She noticed a half-smile as he stooped to pull his shoes off. "That'd be good. Three new baby goats, huh? She's a good little mama, too."

Relieved, she flipped a cornbread johnnycake and stirred the potatoes. "She and Billy Bob sure have helped you increase your goat herd."

She filled their glasses and turned to set the table when his strong arms embraced her. She looked up into the brown eyes that had attracted her when he started attending Grace Community Church more than five years ago. What happened to the dark-headed handsome man she had fallen in love with?

How could a person act one way in public and a completely different way in private? She surrendered to the embrace. She would choose to love him even when she didn't feel love. Love is a choice, she reminded herself as he nuzzled her neck and pulled her closer.

"Let me turn off the stove," she whispered. "I don't want supper to burn." He led her into the bedroom, and she spoke words of love that were lies and submitted to a love she didn't feel. With God's help, she would choose to love this man who made her feel unlovable.

SEVEN

*A*s usual, during the Sunday morning service, Thomas went to check on things, as he called it, and Lillian made her way to the restroom where Kora waited.

"Did he find out you weren't home Wednesday?" Kora asked.

"No, but he almost did. The insurance agent called and told him no one answered the phone. I told him I was outside, which wasn't a lie. I was outside." They laughed, and then both became serious.

"I'm afraid of what he might do if he finds out." Kora hugged her new friend.

"I can handle anything he dishes out," Lillian said. "But I still hope he doesn't. It's painful when he yells at me and even worse when he puts me down and accuses me of cheating or lying. I feel so worthless."

"Nathan did that to me last night," Kora said. "He accused me of cheating on him and called me a whore." She wrinkled her nose and blinked hard.

Lillian hugged her again. "Hang in there, girl. At least we can encourage and help each other. We need to meet during the week so Pastor Bill doesn't start thinking we don't like his sermons. We can't keep leaving every Sunday when he starts preaching."

Kora giggled. "No, we don't want that. I enjoy his messages. But I hate you having to walk three miles to my house. This week, I'll walk to yours."

Lillian pumped some hand lotion into her hand and rubbed it in. "We need a place in the middle." She brightened. "I know. There's a little wooded area about halfway between our houses. I noticed it the other day when I went to your house. I don't walk on the highway because I don't want anyone to see me and offer me a ride. Thomas would hear of that for sure. It's a nice spot just a little way from the highway. As long as the weather is good, we could meet there. Take a sack lunch and have a picnic."

"That sounds wonderful." Kora clasped her hands together. "If it's raining, we may have to skip a week, but maybe that won't be often."

Lillian started to speak when a commode flushed. With bugged-out eyes, they looked at each other and then at a woman coming out of a stall.

"Excuse me," the woman said. She looked guilty. "I'm sorry. I couldn't help overhearing your conversation. I didn't mean to eavesdrop, but I guess that's what I did."

Lillian put her hands to her hot face as Kora backed up against the wall. "I guess we shouldn't have had such a private conversation without checking the stalls," Lillian said.

"May I say something?" The woman glanced at each of the women facing her. "I'm Bella Sharpe. I'm new here. Sounds like your husbands are a little like mine, so I can relate to what you're going through."

"Really?" Kora made a step forward. "Is your husband a jealous and manipulative bully? Ours are."

Bella flushed. "Well, he doesn't quite fit that description, but he's as cranky as a bear and mean as a crocodile. Sometimes, I want to hang him in the rafters by his thumbs and leave him there a day or two."

Lillian looked at Kora and laughed. "Sounds like Bella needs to join us." She turned to Bella. "Kora and I plan to meet during the week to talk and encourage each other. Want to join us?"

Bella smiled. "I'd love to. Except I work Tuesdays and Thursdays at the hospital."

"No problem," Kora said. "We've decided to meet on Wednesdays."

They filled her in and hurried out in time to hear the dismissal prayer at the end of the service.

Thomas stood by the door, watching them. He took Lillian's arm and squeezed it hard. "Where have you been?"

She winced and jerked her arm away. "In the bathroom. Where else?"

He smiled through gritted teeth and nodded to a parishioner they met. "Don't you ever do that again," he growled.

"You don't want me to go to the bathroom?"

"You know what I mean. People will notice. You're making me look bad."

"Oh heavens! I sure don't want you to look bad in front of your admiring public."

She wrapped her arms around herself, suspecting that trouble awaited when they got in the vehicle. At least he waited until they left the parking lot before he blasted her.

He cursed as he pulled out onto the highway. "You witch. I try to make a good impression at that church, and you act like an immature teenager, running to the bathroom to meet your best friends. I assume those floozies are your best friends."

"Thomas, they're just ladies who were in the restroom. And how can I even know them? Because of you, I don't have friends."

He castigated her until they pulled into the drive at home. She slammed the truck door, ran into the house, and threw the meal she had prepared onto the table. Today, he would have to do without corn and bread. Then, she barricaded herself in the spare bedroom. She shuddered as she picked up a book she had placed on the dresser. "Dear Lord, how long?" she prayed. "I know you love me, but I'm beginning to feel so unlovable. I hate what my life has become." She wiped her tears and spent the afternoon immersed in the life of a woman spy during WWII.

About dusk, a knock sounded on the door. She neared the end of the story and didn't want to put the book down, so she ignored the sound. A harder knock followed by two soft ones sounded.

"Lillian, are you okay?"

She turned the page. If only he would let her finish.

"Lillian? Will you come out now? I'm sorry I was so rough with you."

She tried to read faster but had to go back to reread a paragraph. If he would just leave her alone.

"Lillian!" Louder. She didn't want him to get angry again. He might hurt her this time.

"I'm coming. Give me a minute."

"Come on, Lillian. I want to apologize to you. Please?"

"I need to finish a couple of pages of my book. Then I'll come out. I promise."

"Okay. But hurry."

She finished the story and opened the door. He stood grinning, holding a silver gift-wrapped box with a glittery gold-colored bow.

She looked past him into the kitchen, where two place settings and half-burned candles sat on the table.

"What's this?" she asked. She whirled around, almost bumping into him.

"I made us dinner. Your favorite—lasagna and salad. It may be cold by now." He pressed the gift into her hands. "This is for you."

She took the gift and looked up at him. "Why?"

He shifted from one foot to the other. "I'm sorry, Lillian. I'm sorry I yelled at you. But…."

"But what?"

He rushed. "You make me so angry. Why do you do that? You know I…."

She shoved the gift at him. "Never mind. You aren't apologizing. You're justifying yourself for being mean to me. There's no excuse for that."

His face reddened, and his eyes snapped. "I am apologizing. I can't help it if you don't accept it." He shoved her against the wall. "I don't know why I married you when I could have had Victoria." He sneered. "She still wants me, you know. I see it in her eyes."

Inside, Lillian boiled. Beautiful, wealthy Victoria, who started attending church right after Thomas joined, tried her best to get Thomas to marry her and was furious when he married Lillian instead. After that, she took every opportunity to flirt with him, even when Lillian stood right beside him.

Lillian forced herself to stay calm. "I'm sure you can see it in other ways besides just her eyes. She flaunts her whole body at you every time she sees you." She tsked. "If that's what you want, I won't stop you." She extended her hand, palm up. "I married you because I thought you loved me. If you want Victoria, then I won't stand in your way. And what you see in her eyes? That's pure lust, not love. There's one thing I've learned. Love is all about giving, but lust is all about getting."

"What's that supposed to mean?"

"One day, you'll understand." She turned and started to exit the room when he pushed her once more and stalked out the door. She stumbled to the table and sat down. The lasagna and salad, under different circumstances, would have been delicious, but now they were tasteless. The kitchen mess would still be there when she got up. Oh, well. She would take a sleeping pill tonight and stay in the guest bedroom.

Thomas knocked on the bedroom door. "Aren't you coming to bed with me?"

"I think I'll stay in here tonight," she answered.

After a few moments of silence, she could hear the contempt in his voice. "Do what you want, then. I really don't care. I'll probably sleep better and won't have to smell your nasty breath in the morning."

Her breath caught in her throat. If only she could have known this about him before she spoke those marriage vows. She tossed and turned until the twisted bed covers fell onto the floor. Every time she started to drowse, the memory of his hand stinging her face or his mocking words criticizing something she said or did rose like a fresh smack in the face. With every thought, she flipped over to the other side. She rose and remade the bed, then crawled back in. She finally cried herself to sleep.

She slept late the next morning. She was surprised to see a neat and clean kitchen. She gasped. She couldn't believe she had slept so late. Thomas must have cleaned it last night. She wondered if he had skipped breakfast or cooked it himself. He hadn't done that since they married. Since she didn't work outside the home, she accepted his argument that she would do all the housework. She may as well accept it, since he wouldn't agree to any other arrangement.

EIGHT

On Wednesday, Lillian arrived early at the spot she, Kora, and Bella had agreed on. She cleared sticks and rocks from the ground beside a log, spread out an old quilt, and waited for the two younger women to join her. Large oak and maple trees made a canopy over the place, and a squirrel chattered at her for interrupting his nap — if squirrels took naps, which she doubted. Someone once said that all squirrels had ADHD. She didn't doubt that.

Kora and Bella arrived together, chatting like old friends. Kora carried a container of iced tea, and Bella brought a box of chocolate chip cookies. Lillian spread a small tablecloth in the middle of the quilt, and they arranged sandwiches and chips on it.

"I haven't had a real picnic for so long I forgot what it's like," Lillian said.

"I love picnics." Bella filled her travel mug. "Levi and I used to picnic a lot. We used to go to the park with a picnic lunch when we were dating, and when the kids were big enough, we'd take them camping overnight at the river. I loved doing that." She gazed at the clear, blue sky. "I miss it."

"That sounds fun." Kora chased a bite of ham sandwich with a swig of cold tea, picked up an oak leaf, and twirled it in her fingers.

"Something bothering you, Kora?" Bella asked.

"Do your men encourage you when you're beating yourself up over something?"

"Are you serious?" Bella laughed. "My man never knows I'm beating myself up. He isn't aware of my feelings at all."

"What has happened?" Lillian asked.

"Yesterday I could hardly stand myself because I forgot to send a birthday card to Nathan's mom. Two days ago she had a birthday. I usually make her a cake, but it just slipped my mind." Kora rubbed her nose. "I beat myself up about it, and he said, 'You ought to be ashamed. She only has one birthday a year.' He made me feel so bad I cried for an hour. Then I called his mom to apologize, and she persuaded me to come see her to get a hug. He wouldn't even go with me, but she and I had a good visit. I'm glad he didn't go."

"Seems like our men can find plenty of ways to make us look down on ourselves," Bella said. "At least his mom isn't like that. Sounds like a sweet woman and a good mother-in-law."

Lillian tilted her head. "I wonder — do I try to encourage my husband when he needs it? I'll have to think about that."

"Ah, shoot," Bella said. "I'm so busy trying to keep my head clear I know I don't show concern about his feelings. Sometimes I wonder if he feels anything. That's bad, isn't it?"

"I'm afraid I do the same thing. This week I'm going to try to be aware of Thomas's feelings and encourage him." Lillian said.

Bella lifted a finger. "Me, too."

"And me," Kora said.

"Sounds like an assignment," said Bella. "Say, did you hear Mrs. Nell talking to Hank at church Sunday? She told him his guitar sounded out of tune. I thought he would hit the ceiling. He said she was the one out of tune. He said her singing sounded like a frog in a hailstorm. They may have tied up if Pastor Bill hadn't intervened at that moment." She threw her head back and laughed. "I sorta wish Pastor Bill hadn't stopped them. That would have been hilarious."

Kora laughed, and Lillian smiled. Kora peered at Lillian. "You're quiet today, Lillian," she said. "Something happen last night or this morning?"

Lillian crumbled a potato chip and tossed it on the ground. She shook her head and looked up at the leaves above her. "Oh, just the usual. I made my wonderful husband look bad in front of his public, which is a big no-no."

"Oh, my heavens!" Kora wrinkled her nose. "You didn't! How dare you?"

Lillian's lips curved into a half smile. "I did. Of course, he apologized after he made me feel like an idiot. Except it wasn't an apology. It was my fault, he said, for making him so mad. He made me a nice lasagna meal with lit candles and everything."

"Did you eat it?"

Lillian scoffed. "No, I just made him angrier, and he left." She told them what happened. "But do you know what he did? He cleaned the whole kitchen. Shocked me but good! That isn't like him."

"Wow!" Kora said. "Maybe that's a step in the right direction. Could be he's seeing the light and realizing how hard his life would be without you."

Lillian snickered. "Could be he thinks he'd be better off without me."

Bella flicked an ant off the quilt. "Who can figure out these men," she said.

Lillian handed Bella a cookie. "Bella, we don't know your situation. You described your husband as a grouch. Is he really that bad?"

Bella picked out the chocolate chips from her cookie, ate them, and threw away the rest. "He's not so bad if he would stop grouching about everything and being such a slob. And if he would help around the house. He works hard at his job, and then comes home to collapse on the couch in front of the TV for the rest of the day. It doesn't faze him that I come home from work and face all the housework alone. Sure, I work only two days a week, but keeping the house for him and the kids is a full-time job. He could help me on the days I work."

Kora sighed. "At least we aren't required to do two jobs, are we, Lillian? I don't know which is worse, having two jobs or being denied the right to have a job you want."

Bella wrinkled her nose. "I think I have it better than the two of you. I'd hate to live under a dictator. That would be a real turnoff."

Lillian giggled. "It sure is. It's hard to make love with someone who's mean to you one minute and wants to be intimate the next."

Bella lowered her head and looked up at Lillian. "Or someone who never says I love you."

"My man tells me he loves me," said Kora, "right after he slaps me around. He claims he hits me because he loves me. Imagine that."

"Thomas is good at making love," Lillian said. "At least I have that."

"Shoot. Levi doesn't know what foreplay is. He skips that and goes straight to the main course." Bella snapped her fingers in a zig zag motion and wobbled her head. "No appetizers tonight!"

Kora groaned, and Lillian laughed. "Bless your little heart," Lillian said. Then she sobered. "I have been praying for my husband to change. I know God hears me."

"But it's his choice, isn't it?" Bella asked. "I mean, God will talk to someone about their behavior, but he won't force them to change, will He?"

Kora shook her head. "We are free to make our own choices. Pastor Bill says we're free moral agents, and God won't override our will."

"I've been thinking a lot about it," said Lillian. "I journaled my thoughts about it last night."

"I journal sometimes," Bella said. "Not often enough, though."

"You should every day." Lillian pulled out her small floral book. "It really does help me to write my thoughts and feelings down."

"You mean we should write our feelings and thoughts in a notebook?" Kora shook her head. "I'm afraid Nathan will find it and read it. Then he'd really be mad because sometimes I feel like hurting him, like he hurts me. Sometimes my thoughts and feelings toward him are absolutely dangerous. Or would be if I acted on them."

"I used to write them," said Lillian, "but I don't write my real feelings anymore. I write some things, but of course not my feelings and thoughts about my situation. I'm afraid Thomas will read it. I just write about other things."

"I've got an idea," Kora sat up straight. "I think I'll get a notebook and make up stuff."

"Oh, that sounds like fun," Bella said. "I like to make up stories."

"Let's bring our journals and read them to each other," Kora said. They all agreed as they left the little clearing in the woods.

NINE

"Drat! I'm out of brown sugar." Kora had planned a whole meal around a new recipe she found but it called for light brown sugar. Oh well, she'd have to find a different recipe.

She flipped through the recipe book, but nothing sounded good. Why not just go to the store and get what she needed? That's what she used to do. Nathan had never told her she couldn't go to the store, but every time she did, he gave her the third degree, asking who she saw, where she went, and on and on. She hated that, so she seldom went anywhere without him.

She slipped on her shoes, grabbed her purse, and headed out the door. It wouldn't take long to walk to the store. She'd be back in plenty of time to make the meal, and Nathan would never know.

The walk was short, and she enjoyed getting out on the warm sunny day. Sometimes she walked a few blocks around the neighborhood for exercise, but Harps was several blocks away. She stopped to talk to a neighbor a few minutes and waved at a woman she previously worked with.

When she arrived at the grocery, she grabbed a cart and started moving up and down the aisles. She hadn't been shopping alone in such a long time, she enjoyed looking at all the items lining the shelves. She slowed down to enjoy the aroma of the laundry detergents and fabric softeners before she moved to the aisle with the sugar. Then someone called her name. She turned to look into the face of one of Nathan's co-workers.

"Hello, Kora. How nice to see you. It's been a while. How are you?" The man grinned at her.

"Hi, Hank." Kora swallowed hard. "I'm good. You doing okay?" Hank would surely tell Nathan he met her. She dared not ask him not to tell Nathan. What could she do? He asked her about her family and mentioned his surprise at Nathan's promotion.

"Don't get me wrong, I'm glad he got the promotion, but I expected it would go to Sam 'cause he's been there longer. I guess ole Nathan boot-licked his way to the top."

Kora frowned. "Why do you think that? You don't think Nathan deserved the promotion?"

Hank blushed. "Well, yeah, I guess he did. It's just that he doesn't have that much seniority. He's one of the youngest guys there. But I'm happy he's doing so well. He is a hard worker."

"Yes, he is. I'm sure he deserved the promotion, or he wouldn't have gotten it."

"Hey, now, you have a good day. I'll tell Nathan I ran into you."

She grabbed a cake mix from the shelf and held it up. "Please don't—it will spoil my surprise."

He laughed. "Oh. Okay, I won't say a word." He put his finger over his lips to reassure her he would keep her secret, and she waved as she guided her cart down the aisle. Whew! Maybe it would work. She grabbed the brown sugar and headed toward the checkout.

As she waited in the checkout line, she saw a couple she and Nathan had known before they married. The couple had moved to another part of the state, so she hadn't seen them since the wedding.

"Kora!" The woman ran to hug her. "How nice to see you

again. It's been a long time."

"Hello, Nikki. Hi, Trent. So nice to see you again," she said.

They asked about Nathan and chatted until Kora stood next in the line. When she paid for her item and started toward the door, Trent called out.

"Tell Nathan hello. I'd like to see him."

"Yes," Nikki said. "Let's get together soon. Let's exchange phone numbers so we can make a date later and have dinner or something."

Kora looked at the time on her phone as she entered the number, and then she waved and fled. She did not expect these encounters that very well could expose her trip into town.

When Nathan arrived home, she greeted him with a kiss and the surprise dessert she had made. He brushed her aside and went into the bathroom to wash up. When he returned to the kitchen, she had supper on the table.

"Did you have a good day?" she asked. He shrugged and looked sideways at her.

"I think a better question is, how was your day? What'd you do today?"

"Not much," she said. "Worked in the yard a little. As you can see, I made you a special dessert."

"A little birdie told me you took a trip to the grocery store. Why didn't you tell me about that?"

Her heart fluttered. She dreaded the interrogation that would follow. She had done nothing wrong, so why did she feel the need to defend herself? "I didn't think it was important. I needed some brown sugar for the recipe, so I went to get some. That's it."

"Oh yeah? That's not what I heard."

She straightened her back and lifted her chin. "I don't know what you heard or who is reporting on my actions, and I don't care. I don't have to defend myself for going to the store."

"It just happens that I ran into the Harps clerk at the gas

station on the way home. She told me you were talking to some people she didn't know," he said through gritted teeth. "She also said you talked to a man before that. Just who were these people?"

"Oh, so you have spies keeping track of me? How nice." She seethed with indignation. "Do they report every time I go check the mail? Do you have cameras in the house to watch me go to the bathroom?"

"Never mind, Kora. Who were you talking to?"

"Your spy friend should know your friend, Hank, who said to say hi. And the Coopers, Trent and Nikki. You remember them from our dating days, right? They want to see you. They said they'd call later so we could go to dinner or something. Did your friend tell you what I bought?" She picked up the brown sugar and waved it in front of his face.

"We're not about to go to dinner or anywhere else with the Coopers." His stormy eyes bored into hers. "I guess you had a nice chat with Hank, huh? You'd better stay away from that man. That's why I don't like you going out. I know your friendly encounters are more rich than friendly." He stabbed a piece of meat with his fork and poked it into his mouth. His frown deepened, and she imagined his thoughts were filled with visions of her flirting with a room full of handsome men.

She jumped to her feet and threw down her napkin. "Nathan, I'm a grown woman, and I love you and only you. I don't understand why you always think the worst of me. I don't flirt with every man I see, and I'm not doing anything wrong. I hate the implication that I can't be trusted. I don't treat you that way, and I don't appreciate you treating me like that. Please stop."

His eyes widened, and his mouth opened. She whirled and left him sitting with his food half eaten. She stayed in the bathroom until the back door slammed.

She wiped her eyes and pulled out her journal.

Dear Journal: When I first married my wonderful husband, I thought I had the world by the tail. I dreamed of us doing great things together—us becoming successful at our jobs, having a family, living a dream life. Oh well, maybe it can still happen.

Right now, I'd like to just feel loved like I did at first. Actually, not that long ago. What has happened? How can things change so fast? How can one person make another person feel so stupid and inane? So useless? First, he made me feel like a queen, but now he makes me feel like a dunce. Do I make him feel that way? I sure hope not. I would never want to make anyone feel like that. I don't understand how anyone can do that to another person.

Lord, please help me know how to handle this. I so want things to go back to like they used to be.

TEN

At the next week's meeting, Lillian arrived early again and prepared the place for her friends who arrived within a few minutes.

"What in the world happened to you?" Bella pushed back Kora's hair to show a black eye. "What are those marks on your neck? Did Nathan do this to you?"

Kora lowered her head. "It's my fault," she said. "I shouldn't have made him so angry."

"Tell me what happened." Lillian checked the bruises on her face and neck.

"I answered the phone when it rang. Jerry from church called to ask if I would help with the youth group activities. Nathan accused me of having an affair with him. Honest, I don't even know Jerry. He has a wife and a kid. I just answered the phone."

Lillian drew in a big breath. "No, Kora, it isn't your fault. You aren't to blame for his bad temper or his jealousy. Don't blame yourself for his meanness."

"I know people at church want me to be involved, and I'd love to, but I can't. They can't know that every time they call or talk to me, it makes Nathan mad, and I suffer." She thought for a minute. "You know, when we first married, I helped with children's church, but it seemed to irritate him, so I quit. I guess maybe I shouldn't have given in to him when he started trying to control me, but I didn't realize that's what he was doing."

"That's what happened to me," Lillian said. "It took me a while to see the manipulation and control. By the time I saw it, he scared me when I stood up to him."

"I just hate to be the bad guy at church." Kora bit her lip.

"Me too," said Lillian. She shrugged. "Our dear church friends have no idea what we suffer from their show of love and friendliness. I'm sure they think we're lazy and unchristian when we don't participate in the church work and events."

"Yeah," Bella said. "Last Sunday, when that red-headed lady commented that some people aren't committed to God's work, I thought she meant me." She raised her voice and wagged her head to mimic the lady. "Some folks just come late and leave early and never help with anything. I guess they think God will overlook their lack of commitment." A big sigh followed. "She looked right at me when she said it."

"I know," Kora said. "The sting hit me when Sister Do-Gooder reminded everyone that we don't attend all the church functions. She said only ten percent of church members do all the work at the church, while the other eighty percent do nothing to help. And I know they think I'm not friendly. Last Sunday, I overheard someone say that."

Lillian grinned. "What about the other ten percent?"

"Huh?" Kora wrinkled her nose.

"You said ten percent do all the work and eighty percent do nothing. That amounts to ninety percent. What about the other ten percent?"

"Don't give me a hard time because I can't do math," Kora said.

"Oh, I know!" Bella raised her hand and waved it. "The other ten percent keeps track of what the first ten percent does do and what the eighty percent doesn't do."

Lillian laughed. "Don't worry about it, girls. We do what we can. It feels like they are referring to us because we feel guilty, but we shouldn't feel guilty. God knows we can't help our situations. There are a lot of folks who choose not to commit to help. I guess they don't make church work a priority. That's on them, not us. I want to bake something for dinners and bake sales, but Thomas won't even go to those events. He'd have a fit if I spent money and sent something to sell."

Kora stood up and a wide smile covered her face. "Never mind all that," she said, "I want to read you what I journaled this week." She pulled out the little book and read.

Dear Journal: Today I looked out, and a cardinal and blue jay were arguing. I guess it was an argument because the blue jay squawked and bobbed his head while the cardinal ran around. It reminded me of Nathan and me when we argue, except when Nathan yells, I run in the other direction. I guess he's the blue jay, and I'm the cardinal. Finally, the blue jay ran toward the cardinal and pecked him on the head. The cardinal stood taller and jumped in the middle of the blue jay, his wings flapping wildly. He didn't stop until the blue jay flew away. Yay, cardinal!

"Did you make that up?" asked Bella.

"Yes. Some birds in the backyard gave me the idea."

Lillian laughed. "That's a good story. Did Nathan read it?"

Kora put a hand over her mouth. "I'm sure he did because this morning he acted funny. He looked sideways at me and commented on a red bird in the backyard. I just ignored him, but I couldn't help but laugh. Not in front of him, of course."

"Here's my journal entry from last night. Funny, it's also about birds." Lillian read from her little book.

Dear Journal: Today, I went to the barn to check on the new baby goats and heard a bird screaming. A big, red-tailed hawk soared above the barn, and a little bird chased him. The little bird repeatedly flew around the big bird, attacking him. Once, the little bird landed on the hawk's head and pecked him. The hawk screamed, seemingly unable to defend himself against his tormentor. Finally, the hawk landed on the top of a tree so he could fight against the little pest. It's funny how, while soaring in the sky, the bigger bird couldn't fight off the smaller bird. He had to stop flying to fend for himself. But why did the little bird attack him? I read it happens because the big bird is a predator. He probably bothered the nest of the little bird. It reminded me that size doesn't give us a reason to bully others. Smaller things can stand up for themselves when they have a good reason. Sometimes we smaller 'birds' must protect ourselves against those who want to harm us or our little ones.

Bella and Kora were silent for a while before Kora spoke. "That's good," she said. "Did you make it up?"

"Actually, no. This happened yesterday. I kept thinking about it. I thought there should be a lesson somewhere in it. I pitied the big hawk, but then I wondered why the little bird attacked him. There has to be a reason they do that. So, I looked it up."

"Do you think Thomas read it?" asked Bella.

"I'm not sure, but I think so. The journal lay in a different position this morning. He gave no indication he read it, though."

Kora giggled and twisted her wedding ring on her finger. "I don't think I can stand not knowing if Nathan reads my entries. It's stressing me out."

"It's hard," said Lillian, "but we'll keep writing them. Sooner or later, something will come of it, I'm sure. If nothing else, we can entertain them. Of course, when there's a lesson in what we write, maybe it'll hit home."

Kora's eyes widened. "Yeah! I'll try to think of something that has a lesson. Except I don't think I'm good at that like you, Lillian."

"Sometimes there's a lesson when we don't see it," said Lillian. "We'll just trust the good Lord to help us, and He will."

"I have something I need y'all to help me pray about." Bella shuffled her feet in the leaves. "I'm desperate for an answer."

"You say it," said Kora, "and we'll pray it."

"I've been keeping it to myself all this time, but I think I need to tell y'all." Bella wrung her hands and looked back and forth at her friends who waited with big eyes. "Levi is hooked on porn."

Kora jumped to her feet. "What? Porn?"

Bella put her hands over her face. "He's been watching it for a while now. I hate it. He tries to get me to watch it with him, but I won't." She wiped tears from her face. "Do you think God can change him?"

"Yes, of course, He can," Lillian said. "It may take a while, but we'll pray hard, Bella."

"I'm so afraid," Bella said. "I'm afraid I can't compete with those girls on the videos, and I won't be enough for him. I'm afraid he'll do something bad."

"What are you afraid he'll do?" asked Kora.

Bella shrugged. "I don't know. Maybe have an affair. Or rape someone."

Lillian sucked in a sharp breath. "You don't think he would hurt Addie, do you?"

"No, I'm sure he wouldn't do that. If he did, I'd kill him for sure, or at least hurt him bad."

"You poor dear," said Lillian. "We'll pray hard for him. And for you. Hang in there, and don't lose hope."

ELEVEN

"What's for supper?" Levi came through the back door, took off his boots, and threw them into the corner of the room. This routine never failed to prickle her nerves, but Bella said nothing. She would sweep up the mess later like she always did. Pick up his dirty clothes from where he threw them. Sweep the dried mud from his boots when he tramped through the house. Clean up the spilled coffee, beer cans, and potato chip crumbles from the end table every night. It didn't bother him to walk across the floor with his muddy shoes while she mopped it.

"Fried pork chops with potatoes and corn."

"Cornbread?"

"Of course."

"Good. Did Trevor mow the lawn?"

"Ask him. He's in the living room."

His brow furrowed, and she recognized a storm brewing in his head. She'd seen it too many times before. "I asked you. Don't you know what your son does?" A stream of foul words followed, and he stomped out of the kitchen into the living room. "Trevor, did you mow the lawn?"

"I started to mow it, Dad, but I couldn't get the mower started."

She shook her head as she listened to him chew out the boy.

Trevor had worked more than an hour on the old mower with no success. She should've answered instead of letting him jump on Trevor, but he would have anyway.

She stood in the doorway with her hands on her hips. "Levi, I don't know why you don't get a good mower. That old thing is worn out."

He whirled, and she wished she'd kept her mouth shut. She hated it when a foul mood dominated him. He could be sweet and accommodating, but not today.

"Woman, you know it takes money to buy a new mower. If you'd stop going to Walmart every time you turn around, we might be able to save enough to buy something. I don't know what you spend so much on, anyway."

Heat crept up her neck and over her face. "Oh, just the things we need to run this house. You know, like laundry detergent, toilet paper, and cleaning supplies. Clothes for your growing teenagers." The tension rose in her chest and shoulders. "Not to mention the pork chops, bread, and coffee you're so fond of." She turned and walked back into the kitchen, muttering. "I guess we can live on beans and rice so you can save enough to buy a mower. Of course, you might have enough if you'd quit buying that beer and those expensive cigarettes. You might even live longer."

"What'd you say?" he yelled. "You complaining about my cigarettes? I think you've said enough about that. I'll quit when I'm ready to quit."

Oops! She smirked. At least he doesn't need hearing aids. "Supper's ready," she called. "Get washed up, guys."

After supper, Levi put on his boots. "I'm going to work a while," he said. "The pecan grove needs mowing, so I'm using the tractor mower."

She had soap suds up to her elbows as she scrubbed pots and pans when yelling came from outside. She stepped onto the porch and looked around the house. She saw him running across the middle of the pecan grove. The tractor was still running.

"Open the door," he yelled. She opened the door, and he ran inside, slamming it behind him. She stood on the porch looking around. Something buzzed around her head. Bees! Yellow jackets! She ducked and dodged as they flew around her. One caught in her hair, and she screamed and slapped at it. She slung her hand to knock off a bee and a sharp sting hit her middle finger. She fled into the house and slammed the door. Levi stood at the window, peering out.

"Why'd you do that?" she yelled. "Why'd you leave me out there with the bees?"

He looked sheepish. "I'm sorry," he said. "I guess I didn't think."

She smacked him on the back of the head. "That's a good way to treat your wife." She flung her hand and looked at it.

"Did you get stung?"

"Yes, you goof." She ran to the bathroom for something to ease the pain, and he followed. "What happened?" she asked.

"I mowed over a yellow jacket nest, and they came after me. So, I jumped off the tractor and ran."

"Yeah," she said, "and left me out there with the yellow monsters." She ran her fingers through her hair. "I think I got them all out of my hair. What're you gonna do about the tractor?"

"Will you go turn it off?" He grinned.

"Not on your life. That's your job. I've already suffered enough."

Once again, she whacked him on the shoulder. He laughed, grabbed his hoodie, and headed out the door. She looked through the window as he slowly approached the tractor. He covered his head and slipped on a pair of gloves. He ducked a few times, then jumped on the tractor and drove it to the barn. She opened the back door for him, and he pecked her on the cheek as he walked by her to collapse in his recliner.

Before she went to bed, she wrote a journal entry.

Dear Journal: After I survived the attack of the killer bees, I tried a new dish soap that made so many suds I had difficulty rinsing them off the dishes. It's called Soapy Sudsies. My, what an imagination someone has! Bet whoever named it received a large bonus for their genius.

I should be so creative that I could sell my ideas and be rich. I could develop a shampoo that makes your hair grow an inch a day and call it Wash 'n Grow. Or a chocolate bar that makes you lose weight, and name it ChocoLoss. I know! A computer that automatically knows what you want to order online—a Mind-mercial. Oh, wait! We have that already. How about paper that automatically writes what you think? Insta-Journal. Yep. I think I could be rich.

On another note, I'm thinking about working full-time. The only problem is that I'd have two full-time jobs instead of one and a half. I keep thinking I'll get some help around the house, but it isn't happening yet. I keep praying and hoping.

TWELVE

At the next meeting in the secret clearing, Lillian swallowed the last bite of her ham sandwich and pulled out her orange, purple, and green flowery notebook. "We need to make up some code words to communicate in secret, like at church. Have any ideas?"

The younger women nodded and pulled out their notebooks and pencils. "Good idea," said Kora. "I wanted to tell you Sunday that I might not be here today but didn't get a chance. Thankfully, I am here after all."

"Oh, I'm glad it worked out for you to come," said Bella. "I hadn't thought of what we'd do should something happen."

"It will give us a way to communicate if we need to change our meeting or something," said Lillian. "With code words, we can talk about it at church, and no one will know what we're talking about."

"Oh! That sounds fun. Makes me feel like a kid again." Bella clapped her hands. Kora laughed and pushed Bella backward.

"If we need to change the place of our meetings in case it rains or for some other reason, we could say something like — one day, I hope to go to the Grand Canyon. Or, I want to visit Washington D.C."

"Okay, so the Grand Canyon would be my house," said Lillian, "and Washington, D.C. is Kora's house."

"Houston, Texas, is my house," Bella said. "I used to live

there, you know."

"Yes, and if we need to change the time, we could say something about someone's birthdate or age," Lillian said. "Like, that little girl is ten would mean we're meeting at ten. Or his birthday is in November would mean we'll meet at eleven."

"If we can't meet, we'll just say something like, I can't go out this week."

Kora scribbled in her notebook. "How about if there's an emergency and we need to see each other between meetings?"

"That could happen," Bella said. They were silent for a while. "How about something like I broke a nail."

Lillian nodded. "Yes, that would work. We could use the code word 'broke' and use the code morning or afternoon for the time we want to meet. I broke a nail Wednesday morning means we would meet Wednesday at ten. I broke a nail Tuesday afternoon means we would meet Tuesday at one. For any other time, we'll use the birthday code words."

"So—how about on our phones?" Kora asked. "Nathan's always looking at my phone. I'm afraid he'll take it away from me."

Bella studied for a moment. "Won't the same codes work on our phones?"

"Not necessarily," said Lillian. "Thomas also looks at my phone and questions me about any texts I get. I think it's best if we don't text each other."

"That's probably best," Bella said. "Say, I'm so glad you and Thomas came to the dinner at church last week. Thomas seemed to enjoy himself."

"He did." Lillian grinned. "Pastor Bill told him that all leaders should attend all church events, so now we are to attend all of them. He must look good, you know, and if Pastor Bill wants him to be there, he'll be there. That man! He has to impress his admiring fans."

"At least you get to go now," Bella said. "Doesn't that excite you? I love church dinners. Levi doesn't care if I go as long as I take home leftovers for him."

"Sure," Lillian said. "I love church events. I get to talk to people. I hope to renew some friendships I had before I married Thomas."

"I wish Nathan would attend church with me and go to church dinners," said Kora.

Bella snickered. "One warning about church dinners. Don't eat anything old Edith takes. She's an awful cook, but she thinks everyone loves everything she takes. She takes chicken dumplings to every dinner and stands by her dish to make sure everyone gets some. She'll put them on your plate even if you say you don't want any. People go straight to the trash can to dump them. Then she brags that everyone loves her dumplings so much there's never any left over."

They laughed at Bella's story until Lillian turned to Kora. "Kora," she said, "do you have a journal entry?"

"I sure do." Kora flipped through her notebook. "I made up a story about meeting a wild creature in the woods while I hunted for possum grape vines to make my wreaths." She read.

Dear Journal: Today, while I was gathering vines to make my wreaths, a fat, hairy creature with a long snout nose and big teeth chased me. It growled at me, and I climbed a tree to escape it. It lay down under the tree, trapping me there for an hour. I yelled to wake it up, and it snorted, rooted around the bottom of the tree, and then sat looking at me. Finally, a bigger one came. The two ran off together, and I waited a while to make sure they were gone before I climbed down and returned to the house.

"Did Nathan read it?" asked Bella.

"If he did, he can't ask me about it without telling on himself."

Lillian laughed. "Oh, that's rich. We can write all kinds of stuff, and they can't ask us about it." She pulled out her journal. "Here's one of mine for this week." She read.

Dear Journal: Last night I had a weird dream. I dreamed I floated above the house. I could see everything—a bird's eye view. Cows and goats grazed in the pasture, and chickens scratched in the barn lot. Then I saw something else. A little girl ran around the barn, appearing to look for something. She looked in buckets, under hay bales, and in sacks of feed. She looked so sad and started to cry. Then, a little boy stood beside her, comforting her. She kept pointing toward the house and saying something, but I couldn't understand her.

The little boy shook his head and pointed in the opposite direction. He pulled her toward the road, but she fought him to get to the house. I finally saw the reason for her fright. Fire bellowed out of the windows of the house. I thought she wanted to save someone from inside the burning house, but the boy wouldn't let her, like he wanted to protect her. I wonder what it means. I think the girl was me, but I didn't know the boy. And I wondered about those inside the house.

Kora shivered. "Ooh, that's good. Is it a real dream?"

Lillian shook her head. "Not all of it. I had a similar dream once. I just embellished it."

"You should write books," said Kora. "That's a good story." She turned to Bella. "Read one of yours."

Bella blushed. "I'm not as good a writer as the two of you, but here goes." She opened her journal and read.

Dear Journal: Today, I went outside to pull the weeds from the garden. As I pulled grass from around a tomato vine, a big snake rose up and looked right at me. Red circular shapes covered his brown body. His tongue flickered, and he looked mean. I almost fainted!

"This is not the Garden of Eden," I yelled at him. "And I am not Eve. You can't trick me into believing your lies."

He came closer to me and rose until he looked into my eyes. I was so scared I couldn't move. I swear, he laughed, and suddenly I felt brave. I yelled. "This is my garden. Adam isn't here, and I'm not listening to you." He lowered his head and started crawling away.

I do have authority. I don't have to listen to that wicked voice in my ear telling me to give up—to stand down. To back off. Even in my weakest moments, I am strong. No matter what he says or does to me, I will believe. If I end up having to leave him, I'll know that I am not alone. If my heart breaks in two, I know my Savior will heal it.

She closed her journal and looked at her friends.

"Oh, Bella," Kora said. "That's powerful. Did it really happen?"

Bella shook her head. "No, of course not. But earlier I had been reading in Genesis, and I imagined it could happen."

"That's a great entry," Lillian said. "That gives me chill bumps. I need a copy of that to hang on my bathroom mirror to remind me who I am. You also need to hang it on your mirror. If Levi reads that, it should speak to him."

"He probably won't read it," Bella said. "He doesn't care what I say or do. If he did read it, he'd probably laugh and say something stupid about it."

Lillian peered at her. "You think he doesn't care about you?"

Bella fiddled with her hair. "Why would I think he cares for me? He's so cranky and mean. I don't see any caring in that. So, yeah, I think he doesn't care for me at all. The first year of our marriage was like heaven. He was so loving and sweet. Then, for some reason, he started yelling at me. I don't know what happened. I think it started when he brought home a case of beer and started drinking. I hate it when he drinks, and he's drinking more often. I've thought a lot about it. Maybe I'm doing something wrong. He treats me like I'm his child instead of his wife."

"Nathan does that to me sometimes, and I hate it," said Kora. "But I'll bet Levi still loves you. He's let life get in the way and has forgotten."

Bella grimaced. "How can you forget that you love someone?"

Lillian patted her hand. "I know it seems unreasonable, but isn't it true that we all forget to love sometimes? How often do we forget to show love to others? Even God. We get so busy doing things and stressing that we let life get in the way and forget to accept love or show love."

Bella nodded. "I guess that's true. I hadn't thought of that. I know I'm guilty sometimes."

"I do love Nathan," Kora said. "He has become a stinker, but I still love him. Do you want to know what he did this week?"

"What did he do?" asked Lillian.

"I don't guess I told you that he had to have his wisdom teeth cut out," Kora said. "He had it done in the city. The **anesthesia** pretty much knocked him out, so I got him to lie down in the back seat while I drove home. He thought I didn't know where to go, so he kept getting up to give me instructions. I had to drive with one hand and reach back with the other to shove him back down into the seat. 'You lay down. I'll get us home,' I told him. Good grief! That man. He seems to think I don't know anything."

"Didn't you live there before you guys married?" asked Bella.

"Yes, and I drove all over that place." Kora gestured toward the road. "These roads are like dirt roads compared to where I grew up."

"I think it's in their DNA to have to know more than we do," Lillian said.

THIRTEEN

*L*illian was stacking clean bath towels in the linen closet when Thomas came through the door whistling. She went into the kitchen to meet him, and he grabbed her and whirled her around.

"Guess what! I took off a couple of days so we could go on a weekend trip. Doesn't that make you happy?"

She laughed. "Sure! Where are we going?"

"We're going to Eureka Springs. We're gonna stay in the ghost hotel. Maybe we'll see a ghost."

"Oh. That sounds like fun. What brought this on all of a sudden?"

He pulled back and frowned. "You don't want to go? I told Harry you'd like the idea."

"Harry? What does Harry have to do with it?"

"Harry and June are going and asked if we'd go, so I told him we would. You know Harry, Lillian."

She busied herself preparing dinner. "Yes, your friend from work. I've never met his wife, though."

He picked up a slice of fried squash from the platter and ate it. "Yum. That's good. Is it a problem for you that you don't know her?"

"No, it's just that you made plans for us without discussing it with me. I'm not used to that."

"Oh. I bet your precious Jim always talked to you first before he planned anything."

"Pretty much. We made plans together when the plans involved both of us. It's nice to be included."

He threw another piece of squash he'd picked up onto the counter. "I guess I'll never measure up to your perfect Jim, will I? I'm getting tired of trying."

She turned to him. "Thomas, a trip to Eureka Springs with your friends sounds great. When are we leaving so I can get things packed?"

A smile covered his face. "That's my girl. We're leaving first thing tomorrow morning." He ran a finger down her cheek and kissed her gently. "You know I love you, don't you? Next time I want to do something, I'll try to remember to include you in the planning."

She pecked him on the cheek. "Thanks for that. And I'll try not to compare you to Jim. I know that's hurtful, and I don't expect you to be like him. I love you for you."

"That's good to know." He tweaked her ponytail. "Don't forget to pack a pair of dress pants and dress shirt for me and your pretty yellow dress I like so much. It shows off your tan and those pretty brown eyes. Harry and I want to take our girls to a nice restaurant at least one night."

"Oh, that sounds fun. I'll pack as soon as we finish dinner. I'm putting it on the table now, so get washed up." He laughed and kissed her again.

During dinner they chatted about what they could see and do at Eureka Springs. Early the following day, they met Harry and June at their house. Thomas introduced the two women, and they crawled into the back seat so their husbands could have the front. Before long, Lillian and June were chatting like old friends. Lillian learned that June worked as a receptionist at the courthouse where Thomas worked.

"You need to come to the courthouse once in a while," June said. "I've never seen you there."

Lillian laughed. "I let Thomas take care of our taxes and all that financial stuff," she said. "I'm a homebody."

"I get that," June said. "Maybe we can meet for lunch one day."

Thomas glanced back. "I keep her busy at home," he said.

June laughed. "Oh, I'm sure she has time one day to have lunch with me. You can't keep her busy all day, every day."

His look told Lillian that he would never approve of her having lunch with anyone. At least she'd found a way to get out to meet her friends without him knowing. He couldn't control what she did after he left for work. Or could he?

June leaned over toward Lillian. "I love those earrings," she said. "They are gorgeous. Where did you get them?"

"Oh, these." Lillian's fingers went to her ears. "I made them. I like crafting things sometimes."

"What? You made them? How?"

"I made them with resin and rose petals. It's easy. I could make some for you. You can bring me whatever you want them made of, and I will make them." She would offer to show her new friend how but realized she would not be able to spend any time with her after this trip.

They stopped for lunch at a country-style buffet and arrived at the Cresent Hotel later that afternoon. Thomas smiled and attended to Lillian as they checked into their room down the hall from Harry and June. The attention made her happy they had come. The charming rooms were large and furnished with antique dressers and chairs. This would be a good trip for them and, hopefully, one that would heal some wounds in her heart.

She picked up a brochure from the lobby and looked at it. "Oh, Thomas. Look at this. They have a ghost tour and a history tour." She held up the brochure for him to see.

"Yeah. I don't care anything about a tour," he said. He

flipped on the TV and plopped into an armchair. "Isn't it enough that we came? Don't spoil it by wanting to go here and there."

She looked up at him. "But, sweetheart. Think of how much fun it would be to get out and see things while we're here."

"We'll see things. I promised Harry we'd shop with them in the old downtown stores. That ought to be enough to make you happy."

Her shoulders slumped, and she threw the brochure onto the nightstand, her excitement drowned by disappointment. Oh well, at least they were here. She would make the best of it.

"I can't believe you bragged to June about those earrings you made."

"What? I was not bragging. She asked about them, and I told her."

"Well, I call what you did bragging. Telling her you could make some for her. Humpf. You know that isn't Christian."

"What? You can't be serious. I don't know what's un-Christian about offering to make her earrings."

"You're making a fool of yourself and don't even know it. What's the big deal about making a pair of earrings? Anyone could do that. I still say you're bragging. And that, my dear, is un-Christian."

Her face grew hot, and she went into the bathroom. She looked into the mirror at her red face. Why did he always make her feel like she sinned in everything she did? She sure didn't mean to brag. She leaned over and inspected the earrings. No, answering a question and offering to do something nice for another person could not be considered bragging. Maybe anyone could make earrings, but everyone didn't want to.

She went back into the other room to wait on Harry and June. He kept his eyes on the TV and didn't speak. She tried to keep positive thoughts, determined this trip would be fun. Finally, a knock sounded at the door. Thomas didn't even glance away from the TV screen. Lillian answered the door and invited Harry and June in.

"Hey!" Harry slapped Thomas's foot he had stretched across the arm of the chair. "Come on, bud. We didn't come here to watch TV. We came to see this place. To take advantage of this old town. To have fun, man!"

Thomas grinned. "Yeah, okay. I'm ready for whatever you have planned for us. I don't know about Lillian. She's the old stay-inside wet blanket."

Lillian gasped and stared at him. His look warned her not to oppose him. "Oh, I'm ready and willing to have some fun," she said. "What are we doing tonight?" She blushed at June's questioning look and Harry's look of sympathy toward Thomas. If she had to prove she could be a fun person, she would.

June looped her arm around Lillian's. "Girl, we're going to have a blast," she said as she pulled her down the hall. "You'll see. Harry and I have signed up for the ghost and history tours. You and Thomas need to sign up soon before they're full. That way, we can go together."

Lillian looked sideways at Thomas. "Sounds like fun to me," she said.

"Why, of course, we'll sign up." Thomas' voice carried down the hall, causing other residents to look at them. He made a big deal of them signing up for both tours, bragging to everyone around that he could scare any ghost away and that he made straight A's in every history class he had ever taken.

They laughed and talked all through dinner, with Thomas sharing stories of his life as a bachelor while Harry looked envious. June jabbed him with her elbow, reminding him that he loved being married to her. He hugged her and agreed, then urged Thomas to admit that his life had improved since he now had a wife to care for him. Thomas glanced at Lillian.

"Yeah, I have to admit that it is nice to have someone

around to take care of me. I'm afraid I didn't do a good job back then." He put an arm around her and squeezed. "My little wifey keeps everything going at home while I keep everything going elsewhere. I guess it's a trade-off."

June glanced at Lillian with raised eyebrows. Lillian smiled and nodded. "Yes, and it's a good tradeoff. I don't have to worry about paying the bills, and he doesn't have to worry about keeping the house clean or cooking meals. Not bad, I'd say, considering how much a good housekeeper and cook costs nowadays. If we weren't married, I don't know if he could afford me."

Harry laughed, and one side of Thomas' lips raised. She might suffer for the remark later, but she enjoyed it now.

When they returned to the room before the Ghost Tour, Thomas' laughter stopped as soon as the door closed. "I didn't appreciate that crack about me not being able to afford you if we weren't married," he said. "I did okay before we married. I didn't have to have a wife to take care of me, and I had plenty of money."

"Oh, Thomas, I didn't mean anything. I know you are well able to take care of yourself without me. You're smart and a hard worker. Everyone knows that."

"But you made me look bad in front of my friends. I won't have that, and you know it." He flopped down on the bed and turned the TV on. "I don't know if I'm going on the Ghost Tour. You've embarrassed me."

She barely stopped an eye-roll as she sat on the edge of the bed. "Thomas, please don't be angry with me. Don't let a misunderstanding spoil our fun. I'm sorry for what I said." She leaned over to kiss him, but he turned his head. "Won't you please forgive me?"

He rolled away from her. His bottom lip pooched out, and he shook his head. "I don't know if I can. Seems like every time I turn around, you're embarrassing me. I wish we hadn't even come on this trip."

"Okay, then. If you want to pout and be mad, I can't stop you." Lillian stood and went into the bathroom to freshen up her hair and makeup. "I'm going on the Ghost Tour even if you don't. I intend to enjoy myself. I intend to enjoy the whole weekend."

She peeped around so she could see him in the mirror. His stormy face matched his stiff posture, and she cringed. Maybe she shouldn't have said that. Now, he would make sure she didn't enjoy it. "Harry and June will be here soon. Are you ready?"

Thomas jumped up from the bed and turned off the TV. "Oh, I'll go. But don't expect much from me." He uttered a sarcastic laugh. "On the other hand, I'll show you how much fun I can be."

Turning on the charm, he opened the door when Harry tapped. "Hey, you two. We'd about given up on you. We're ready." He rubbed his hands together. "This is gonna be fun."

In a show of tenderness, Thomas placed one hand on the small of Lillian's back as they walked out the door. She looked up at him and smiled, even though she wanted to strangle him.

"You two make such a handsome couple," June said. "You're a good example of romance for the rest of us."

Harry rolled his eyes. "Yeah," he said, "you need to slow down a little, Don Juan. You're makin' me look bad." He put an arm around June's shoulder, and she laughed.

"You keep it up, Thomas," she said. "Harry could use a little help in the romance department."

They opted to take the stairs instead of the elevator to the fourth floor for the tour. While Thomas held Lillian's arm to guide her, Harry held to June's hand, pretending to be afraid. When they reached the tour spot, they joined several others sitting on benches in the hall, waiting for the guide. Thomas continued to be attentive to Lillian, and she had to admit, she enjoyed it immensely. "Why can't he always be like this?" she wondered.

They enjoyed the old pictures and the Air Calliaphone exhibit. The guide told great stories and the history lessons held their attention. Harry entertained the group by pretending to see a ghost when the guide took them to the morgue. Thomas flung himself in front of the ladies to protect them, making June and Lillian giggle.

Toward the end of the tour, Harry, June, and Thomas were chatting with the tour guide when Lillian froze and pointed. At one end of the hall where the lights were dimmer, a small circle of light wobbled and bobbed. "What is that?" she whispered.

Thomas turned to look. He grabbed her arm and backed up. "What is it? Let's get outta here."

Harry and June stopped talking and turned. June gasped, and Harry made a choking noise.

"Uh—what is that?" he said. He rushed past June and Lillian. "I'm gettin' outta here," he whispered. Thomas hovered close behind him.

The guide, who had walked away to speak to others in the group, stepped to one side to allow them to pass. "Where are you going?" he asked.

Harry pointed down the hall, but the light blob had disappeared. "I saw something over there," Harry said. "A circle of light." He shuddered. "Creepy! I don't want to see it again."

The guide laughed. "Oh, you saw an orb. Those are pretty common around here, and yes, they are rather spooky. But they're harmless. We haven't had one attack us yet."

Thomas regained his composure. "It may not attack, but it had ole Harry here sweatin'." He walked back to where Lillian stood. "Are you all right, sweetheart?"

She smiled. "Yes, dear, I'm okay. I'm so glad you were here to protect me." She winked at June, who smothered a snicker.

After the tour, they entered the Sky Bar to enjoy some late-night pizza. A man sitting at a table close to them smiled at Lillian, and the scowl on Thomas' face grew darker. She tried to ignore it, but Thomas bumped her with his elbow when Harry and June weren't looking. He kept an arm around her shoulders and pinched her arm until she cried out.

"What happened?" June asked.

"It's nothing," Lillian said, rubbing her arm. "I bumped my arm on the back of the chair."

"She's just a little clumsy at times," Thomas said. "Dear, you need to be more careful. I don't want you all bruised up."

She gave him a dirty look, and he pinched her again. She wiggled out from under his arm and rose. "I have to use the restroom," she said. June jumped up and followed her.

"Are you all right?" June asked as she looked closely at her face. "Did you hurt your arm?"

"No, I'm fine," Lillian said. "I'm just a little tired, I guess."

June grabbed her arm and looked at it. "Wow, Lillian, you must have hit it pretty hard. It's all red." She lifted the arm higher. "You have some old bruises here."

Lillian pulled her arm away from June and shrugged. "It's okay. Like Thomas said, I can be clumsy. It'll clear up in a day or two."

June frowned. "Are you sure you're okay?"

Lillian laughed. "Yes, I'm sure. Now, let's get back out there and see if we can get our guys to plan another tour or something before this trip ends."

FOURTEEN

*L*illian and June convinced their husbands to visit the Thorncrown Chapel, see the Christ of the Ozarks statue, and later attend the Passion Play. Harry entered Thorncrown Chapel into his phone and looked for street signs.

"There it is!" He pointed.

Thomas turned on the street which wound upward between low-hanging tree branches. They traveled up the steep hill, and when they reached the top, the street leveled off. From the back seat, it looked to Lillian and June like they were driving straight toward the sky. The men laughed at their gasps and teased them about being cowards.

Thorncrown Chapel did not disappoint them. The beautiful glass-covered chapel nestled among the trees, provided visitors with an awe-inspiring scene. Made almost entirely of glass, the tall chapel appeared to be an open-air structure in the middle of the forest.

"Look," June pointed at the brochure. "They do lots of weddings here. This would be the perfect place for a couple to get married. Harry, we could come here to renew our vows on our fiftieth anniversary."

"Yeah, sure." Harry glanced back. "If we make it. We still have a few years to go."

"The way you two are going," Thomas said, "you'll make it without any problem. Now Lillian and I are still newlyweds, so we have much further to go. Right, baby?" He reached back and patted Lillian's knee. She laughed.

They drove further along the highway, enjoying the Ozark scenery. Lillian and June pointed out beautiful flowers and trees they saw beside the road and on the hillsides. Later, they found a restaurant and had lunch, then walked along the streets downtown, stopping to browse in shops and antique stores. June found a painting she wanted, and Lillian longingly touched a statue of a small child holding a kitten.

"This would look good in my flower bed," she whispered.

"Oh, that is adorable," June said. "Go ahead and get it."

Lillian glanced at Thomas who was eyeing a fishing rod. "No, I'd better not," she said. She eased away from the display. June strode over to Thomas and pointed at the statue.

"Thomas, you should get that for Lillian," she said. "It would look great in her flower bed, don't you think? I know she likes it."

Thomas walked over to the display and picked up the statue. "Lillian? Where is she?" June dragged her from the next aisle. "Lillian, do you want this?" he asked. He picked up the statue.

"Oh, no. It's too much," she said.

"If you want it, just say so," he said. "I'll get it for you."

"Well, I do like it. But I don't want you to spend that much on me."

"Darling, you're worth it." He took the statue to the clerk and paid for it. He carried the boxed item to the vehicle and shoved it into the back. She tensed and dreaded what he would say when they were alone. Sure enough, when they were back in their room, he started on her.

"Woman," He said, "is there no end to the money you want me to spend? You know this stuff costs. Are you looking for ways to break me?"

"But Thomas, Thorncrown Chapel and Christ of the Ozarks are free. If you didn't want to go, you should've told me. I'm okay when you don't want to do something."

"You sent June to ask me, didn't you? You knew I couldn't refuse in front of them. That's manipulation, and I don't appreciate it. The Bible says for wives to honor their husbands. If you honored me, you'd ask me before you make plans. That's what you want me to do, right?"

Her face reddened. "No, I didn't know June was going to tell you about the statue. And I do respect you." She picked up her phone. "I'll call them and tell them we're not going to the play."

He snatched her phone out of her hand. "No, you won't. You want me to look bad? I think you'd like that."

"No, Thomas. I don't want you to look bad. You're my husband." She reached a hand to touch his face, and he slapped it down. A jagged sigh shuddered through her body as she entered the bathroom and prepared for bed.

"You sacking out all ready?" he asked. "How can you be sleepy after all the excitement we've had?"

She smiled at him. "It has been fun, hasn't it? But I'm a little tired."

He looked her over. "You don't look tired. In fact, you look good." He rolled over to her side of the bed. "You look so good I can't keep my hands off you." He proceeded to caress her. His mouth found hers, and a passionate kiss followed. She struggled to respond, determined to push down the feelings of anger and rejection that threatened to take over her heart.

After yielding to his passions, she lay awake most of the night. When she finally slept, she dreamed of fighting with a large, black dog with blazing red eyes. She woke feeling drained.

Just as she rolled over and sat up, Thomas yelled from the

bathroom. "What in the world!"

Startled, she jumped up and ran to see why he yelled. There, on the foggy mirror, a simple word had appeared. Change.

His white face contorted. "That word just appeared there. When I started shaving and the mirror fogged up, I saw it. I think a hand wrote it." His eyes were huge.

She looked from him to the message. "You mean — it just appeared?"

"Yes. Like an invisible hand wrote it."

"Wow! That's spooky!"

His hand trembled as he wiped his half-shaven face and backed out of the room. "We're gettin' outta this place, now. The sooner, the better."

Lillian started throwing things into their suitcases. She called June and told her what happened. Harry knocked on the door a few minutes later, and Thomas dragged him into the bathroom to show him the barely visible message.

"I tell you, it was plain," Thomas said. His voice squeaked. "I'm not lying or imagining things. Like a hand wrote the message in the mirror fog. Change, it said."

Harry looked skeptical. "Probably just a fluke," he said. "Probably just looked like a word." He looked closely at the mirror, and his eyes widened. "Wait! I see it."

"Did you see it?" June asked Lillian.

Lillian nodded. "It was plain at first. Just one word — change."

Harry looked from one to the other. "We already have our tickets for the play," he said, "but we can stay somewhere else tonight."

Thomas agreed. "I'm done with this place." He grabbed the bags and practically ran to the vehicle.

They visited the Christ of the Ozarks that afternoon before the play. During the play, Thomas put his arm around her shoulders and patted her. His dimples appeared several times as he smiled at her. At one point, he brushed a tear from his cheek. Lillian sent a silent prayer of thanksgiving up to God.

When they arrived home, a letter without a return address awaited Lillian. She pushed it aside while she put away the luggage and did laundry. When she picked it up, it reeked with the scent of Chenel 05. She opened it and gasped.

Lillian, I want you to know that Thomas is planning to leave you for me, so you may as well save him the trouble and leave him. Victoria

With trembling hands, she wadded up the letter and threw it into the trash. She had to believe God was dealing with Thomas. She had to let Him deal with Victoria. Besides, she could do nothing besides start a scene. That would do more harm than good. If her husband chose to leave her, she could do nothing. Maybe it would be better for her. Unless he changed his behavior toward her, a rough time faced her anyway. She retreated into the bedroom for a good cry.

As they ate the evening meal, Thomas talked about work and even mentioned something about church and Pastor Bill. She forced a smile at him when he asked for a biscuit.

"Thomas, despite the weird things that happened, I enjoyed our trip so much. Thank you for taking me. And your friends are nice. Maybe we could have them for supper one evening."

He scowled. "I don't think so. It's okay to have friends at work, but I don't want to bring them home with me."

She blinked. "I only mean for a meal. Then we could visit and get to know them better."

"Nah. You don't need to get to know them any better. You and June talked enough to do you for two lifetimes." He reached over and flicked her hair. "Aren't I enough for you? I know you're enough for me."

"Well, yes. But Thomas, you see other people every day. I don't see anyone. I get lonely for friends."

His eyebrows pulled together. "Now, Lillian, I understand that, but you know I don't like you sharing our lives with other people. If you had friends, that's what you'd do. Right?"

"I'd like to have friends with whom I could discuss things I find interesting. Women's things. Like cooking and keeping house, and children. All the things women have in common. That's all."

He grinned at her and pushed back his plate. "You are an excellent cook and housekeeper. You don't need help from any other woman. And I'm sure they can do those things without your help." He rose, then leaned over and kissed her on the forehead. "I love you, darlin', and I want you all to myself." He went into the living room, stretched out in his recliner, and flipped on the TV.

She sat for a few moments before she started clearing the table. Jim used to help her do that. Come to think of it, he helped her do almost everything. She missed the camaraderie they shared as they worked together. They'd laughed, joked and discussed good books, movies, and recipes. She cringed and smacked her forehead with the palm of her hand. Enough! She had to stop comparing Thomas to Jim, even in her mind.

She finished cleaning the kitchen and went to join him, but he was leaned back in his recliner, sound asleep. She curled up in her chair and picked up a book. If she couldn't have real live friends, at least she could read about them. Of course, she had Kora and Bella. Her life had been so much better since they'd become friends.

She read a while and then opened her journal. While she dared not write her thoughts, she could make up something to get her mind off the day's events.

Dear Journal: What if—the world ended today? I inherited a

million dollars? A huge pandemic killed everyone in the world except me? I invented something everyone in the world wants and I became rich and famous?

Those are big what ifs. I guess if the world ended today, I wouldn't be here writing in this book. If I inherited (or won) a million dollars, how would I change? I hope I wouldn't, but I think anyone would. Maybe I would get to travel the world. Maybe I would use the money to help needy people. Pay some of their debts so they would be better off. I'm sure I would invest a lot of it, then I could live from the interest.

And if I were the only one left alive on the earth, I have no idea what I'd do. Just try to survive, I guess. Probably search for anyone else who might have survived.

I might someday invent something important. I'm sure there are lots of things still needed in our world.

Having lots of money might change my life, although right now, I can't see how. Being stuck in my present life isn't as bad as being the only person left alive, but I can think of lots of things that would be an improvement.

Dear Lord, help me be more appreciative of my present life. I know you are mindful of me and love me.

A song started in her head and soon came out her mouth — "He knows me now, and he loves me."

FIFTEEN

A few days later, Lillian, Kora, and Bella met in their *lieu de rencontre*, which Bella said meant meeting place in French. They decided to use the term for their spot in the woods.

"Lillian, tell us about your trip," Kora said at their next meeting. "Did you have a good time?"

Lillian smiled. "Yes, I did. There were some tense moments, but I enjoyed it a lot. I enjoyed getting to know Harry and June. She's a wonderful person. I wish we could see more of each other."

"Did you go see the Passion Play?" Kora asked. "I've heard it's really good. I want to go see it someday."

"We did see it, and yes, it's really good--so realistic with all the animals and the authentic settings. I felt like I was there in Jesus' time."

"Didn't y'all stay in the Cresent Hotel? Is it really haunted?" Bella asked.

"I didn't believe so," Lillian said. "I don't believe in ghosts, but when we started on the ghost tour, we saw an orb shining spots on the floor. The guide implied that those are fairly common. I do believe God is moving to answer my prayers, though."

"How's that?" Kora asked. "Did something happen?"

Lillian leaned forward. "Do you remember the story in the

Old Testament when a hand appeared and wrote on the wall? Well, Thomas believes that happened in our room."

While wide-eyed Bella and Kora listened, Lillian told them what had occurred in the hotel's bathroom.

"Oh, my heavens!" Bella exclaimed. "What'd you do?"

"What'd Thomas do?" asked Kora. "Was he scared?"

"Terrified! We packed our bags and got out of there fast."

"I would have, too. How'd Thomas respond to that message?" Kora asked.

"He won't even talk about it," Lillian answered. "Once I started to bring it up, but he shushed me. So, I don't really know how he feels about it. I believe God is working hard on him, so I expect to see a change. I hope it won't take too long, though. I'm trying to be patient."

"Hopefully, things won't get worse before they get better," said Bella. "That's what my granny always said when we prayed about something."

Kora glanced at Lillian. "Weren't you scared? I mean, how spooky for a word to appear on the mirror. I would've been terrified."

Lillian looked at her friends and then looked away. One side of her mouth lifted, and she sighed. "Well, actually, there's more to the story."

"What is it, Lillian?" asked Kora. "There's something you're not telling us."

Lillian put a hand over her mouth to stifle a snicker. "I do have to let you in on a little secret." She snickered again. "Actually, I did it."

"You did what?" Bella asked.

"The word on the mirror. During the night, I visited the bathroom and wrote the word on the mirror with my finger. I didn't think anything else about it until it appeared the next morning when the mirror fogged up. I dared not say anything then."

Kora drew in a sharp breath, and Bella howled with laughter. "Oh, that's priceless!" Bella said between gasps for air. "You managed to give him a message without even intending to. That's great."

"God works in mysterious ways," Kora said. "Now, Thomas thinks God sent him a private message. I guess, in a way, He did."

"Looks like," Lillian said. "Maybe another thing he experienced helped, too. When we were looking for the Christ of the Ozarks statue, we turned on a street that went almost straight up. I've never seen such a steep road. I think Thomas almost had a heart attack. When we got to the top, we could see nothing but trees and sky. Then, when we turned to go back down, it was the same. Trees and sky. Looked like we were driving into thin air."

"I've read that Eureka Springs is a unique town," Kora said.

"It's historical with some great stories. The streets are narrow, and the town is on two levels. It's a pretty place but not the best place to drive. Actually, there's another town below the present town. Years ago, a mudslide buried the first town, and the people built another town on top of it. There are places you can see parts of the first town under the stores through vents in the sidewalk. I think there's a tour you can take to see parts of the buried town."

"Really? I'd love to see that," said Bella. "Maybe one day Levi and I can visit there."

"I want to go, too," said Kora. "One day, Nathan will stop his craziness, and we can go places and do things."

"We're believing for that," said Lillian. "And we'll keep believing until it happens."

"Yes, we will," Kora said. "Before we leave, I have started to journal, and I'd like to read something I wrote." She pulled out her little notebook.

Dear Journal: Today, I decided to change. Change my hair,

change my clothes, and change my mind. It's a big deal to me, because I don't like change.

I'm going to part my hair on the opposite side just because it's my hair and I can if I choose. All my life, I've parted it on the right side, but now I'll part it on the left. The only problem I have is, my hair doesn't want to part on the left. Maybe I'll comb it straight back.

I'm going to change my clothes. When I look in my closet, I don't like my clothes anymore. I may start dressing in a more modern fashion. Ditch the jeans and start wearing trousers. Or maybe more casual, like sweatpants. The trouble with that is, I'm not allowed enough allowance to buy new clothes. Maybe I can find another person my size to swap with. I wonder if anyone would agree to that.

I'm also changing my mind. I used to consider myself an intelligent, free, independent woman. I know now that isn't true. I'm none of these anymore, and I don't know how to get my independence back. Lord, help me.

She closed the notebook and looked at her friends who were staring at her.

"Oh, Kora." Bella put her hand over her mouth. "Bless your heart."

"My sweet friend," Lillian said. "It's clear things are hard for you. I wish I could do something to help. All I know to do is pray and be your friend."

Kora nodded. "Thank you, ladies. It helps to have understanding friends who are there for me. I'll get through this somehow with God's help."

Bella sniffed. "We all will. I'm so glad I met you girls. It really does help when we meet and encourage one another. I know God is mindful of our predicaments and will help us."

They hugged, prayed together, and left.

SIXTEEN

After Thomas ate his usual breakfast, he picked up the bowl of goodies Lillian had prepared for him to take to work. He raised the lid and sniffed the cinnamon and chocolate goodies. "Ummmm!" he uttered. "They smell heavenly." Often, he shared the cookies and candies Lillian loved to bake with those who worked in the courthouse near his office. He pecked her on the cheek.

"I'm in a hurry," he said. "I need to get to the office early to fill out some paperwork." He gave her another peck on the cheek. "Got a busy day planned?"

"Not really. Just the usual cleaning ritual I do every day. Plus, water the animals and check on the little goats." Lillian returned his kiss and grinned. "I'm thinking about taking a trip to South Texas to visit the Alamo. That seems like an interesting historical place, and I like history."

He slapped her on the butt. "You behave yourself. Don't forget to check on ole Betsy. She could calf any day now. I'll see you at supper." He lifted the container. "Everyone at the office will be happy to see these. Thanks for making treats for them." He embraced her and planted a lusty kiss on her mouth. Then, he touched her lips. "And remember, these are for me alone."

As he backed up his truck, Lillian stood on the porch, waving. Just as he started to drive forward, she turned her back, pulled down her pants, and then jerked them back up. His eyes were about as wide as his open mouth. He slammed the brake and rolled down the window.

"You mooned me!" he yelled. "I can't believe you mooned me!"

Feigning shock, she waved to him. His head jerked around, and he stomped the gas pedal and spun out. She cringed. Looked like her playful spur-of-the-moment joke made him mad. Oh, well, it wasn't the first time she made him angry. He could get over it. Like her mom used to say, he's got the same clothes to get glad in. She went back into the house to see what he'd put on the duty list for her to do. While she washed the dishes, she rolled her eyes and giggled. She would not share this caper with her friends.

Soon after lunchtime, she went to the barn to check on Betsy. She couldn't locate the cow, and that concerned her. She looked behind the barn, in the lot, and all around. No Betsy. Where could she be? She rubbed her forehead and started for the woods behind the barn. She leaned over to push through honeysuckle vines and brambles. Nothing. She looked behind trees. She climbed hills and waded a cold creek. Still nothing. She sat down to rest on a pile of pine needles.

"What am I going to do? Where could that crazy cow be." Wait! A sound like a moo reached her ears. Then she heard it again. She jumped up and followed the sound. There, in the bottom of a gully, Betsy stood licking a tiny replica of herself.

Lillian slid down the embankment and made her way to the pair. "Betsy, what am I going to do with you? Why did you come way out here to have your baby? How am I going to get the two of you back to the barn?" Betsy looked at her as if to say she had confidence Lillian would take care of her baby.

Lillian looked around. She probably could not carry the calf over the hills, through the brush, and across the fields to the barn. She was strong, but not that strong. Remembering war movies she'd viewed in the past, she pulled honeysuckle vines from bushes and trees until she had enough to create a sort of stretcher. Then she laid the baby calf on top and tied it on with some vines. She hoped Betsy would follow her baby.

She dragged her load to the end of the gully and grunted as she tugged it over a small hill. Sweat ran into her eyes, and she stopped to catch her breath. From there, she could see the field that lay between the woods and the barn. She must have gone in circles when she came to find Betsy, because this way seemed much shorter. By the time she arrived at the barn with the animals, she gasped for breath and her clothes were soaked with sweat. She went inside, took a shower, and rested in Thomas' recliner until time to make supper.

When he returned from work that evening, Thomas still fumed. He came into the house, threw his briefcase on the counter, and glared at her.

"What in the world do you mean exposing yourself right out in the open like that? Don't you know someone might be looking? Is that what you want? Someone to see your nakedness?"

"Thomas, there's no one out here. No one can see from the road — it's on the other side of the house. I meant my nakedness only for you." She laughed, trying to get him to lighten up. But she soon realized he wouldn't lighten up. Her prank backfired.

He grabbed her arm and shoved her into a chair. He leaned over her, and spittle covered her face as he bellowed at her. "There might have been a hunter in the woods over there," he yelled. "You never know when someone might be walking around and see you. Do you do that while I'm gone? Do you run around here naked for everyone to see?"

"Of course not." She wiped her face and inhaled sharply. Maybe her little caper wasn't the wisest thing she could have done. "I would never show myself to anyone except you. I only wanted to make you smile. I wanted to see your dimples." She cut her eyes up at him. "You know those dimples turn me on."

He pulled back. "Well, from now on, do that inside the house, not outside." When he huffed out of the room, she drew in her breath and raised her voice. "Betsy had her baby today. Looks just like her."

"What?" He hurried back into the kitchen. "What did you say? Betsy had her calf?"

She nodded and started to set supper on the table.

"Well? What happened? Are they all right? Where are they?"

"In the barn." The aroma of food filled the kitchen as she poured corn into a bowl and set it on the table.

He blew out his breath and turned a circle. "Are you sure they're okay? Did she have it in the barn?"

"Hardly." She ladled potatoes into another bowl and placed it on the table beside the corn. "She had it in the woods."

"In the woods? Where?" He squeaked, his eyes wide.

She put the back of her hand on her forehead. "In a gully. Back behind the barn. Over the hill a little way from the field."

He sat down hard in a chair. "Not far? The barn is a long way from the woods." He rubbed his chin. "Did you bring them home? How?"

She finished putting the food on the table and sat down. Then, she explained her method of bringing home a cow and her baby. His eyes stayed on her face as she talked, and she gestured as she described the process. "I named the baby Honeysuckle," she said.

"That's unbelievable," he said when she finished her story. "I can't believe you did that. You are an amazing woman, you know that? Amazing. And you named it Honeysuckle?"

She nodded and grinned as they ate and hummed as she cleaned the kitchen. The rest of the evening, while he sat in front of the TV, he kept shaking his head and glancing at her. She had scored a point with him for once.

She smiled and wrote in her journal.

Dear Journal: Sometimes I'm an idiot. How could I do something so foolish? Guess I'll never moon my hubby again, even though it was pretty funny. At least I thought so, even if he didn't. But it's okay now. I may be a hero since I rescued Betsy and her baby.

On another note, I saw the cutest thing today. A stripped stray mama cat with a tiny gray baby kitten came into the yard. The baby looked like a furry gray ball. I know they were hungry, and someone once told me (I won't say who!) to never feed stray animals or they'll stay. But I couldn't help myself. How could I let these little creatures starve when I have plenty of food? So, I put out some milk and bread. The mama cat ate a little, then she pushed the baby kitten up to the bowl with her nose. She let the kitten eat all it wanted before she took another bite. That's what I call a caring parent. She cared enough about her baby to put it before herself.

I wish more people in the world were like that. There are so many stories about abusive parents and children who are neglected. Sometimes I'd like to gather up all the abused and neglected children and bring them home with me. Can't though. Just have to pray for someone to care for them.

And the cats? I think they've made a home in our barn now. I named the Mama Genie for Generous and the Baby Gravy. I'll put some food out for them. Maybe no one will be the wiser.

SEVENTEEN

After Kora kissed Nathan and waved as he left for work, she turned to start her day as a housewife. That's the way she thought of herself. Housewife. The house's wife. Not a stay-at-home mom. She wasn't a mom. Just a housewife.

She looked around the living room and then walked into the kitchen. The breakfast dishes were in the sink, and grease covered the stove. She thought of the job she previously had at the bank. She loved having an office of her own, working closely with people, and making her own money. She didn't mind housekeeping, but that's not what she'd planned to do all her life. As a child, she had dreamed of being the CEO of a business and working in one of those tall buildings in the city. She would have been good at it, too. She had a brain for working with money and handling business matters. Hadn't she handled their finances when Nathan and she first married? She remembered when he bragged about her to his parents after she acquired their new home at a bargain price and handled all the financing. She couldn't stop smiling for a week after that.

She finished the cleaning and went to the yard to pull some weeds from a flower bed. She guessed her green thumb came from her mom who loved raising flowers. She cradled a purple iris and smelled a pink rose. Hmmm. She touched a white and orange lily. More of them would bloom soon. Hen and chicken succulents spilled over from a pot she had found at a flea market before Nathan cracked down on her activities. At least, now she had plenty of time to work in her flowers.

A honeybee buzzed around her hands as she handled the delicate blossoms. She laughed. "I'm not stealing your pollen," she said to the little creature. "You take all you need."

A hummingbird flitted around some tall, blue delphinium she had planted last year. A red-throated hummer chased a tiny brown one from a feeder she'd hung in the shade of a redbud tree in the middle of the yard. "You little bully," she scolded the bird. "There's enough for you and ten more." Why did some creatures bully others? Like Nathan. Why had he turned out to be such a bully? When they first married, he treated her like a queen.

She rose and brushed dirt from her knees. Anger boiled up inside, and she slammed the door as she went into the kitchen. She jerked open the refrigerator and pulled out some leftover pasta. After she ate, her stomach rumbled. She downed an antacid and looked at the empty pasta bowl. What about that food upset her stomach? No, it wasn't the food. The anger caused her stomach to be upset. Every time her emotions boiled over, so did her stomach. She could blame her stomach problems on Nathan. Maybe he needed to experience an upset stomach for a change.

Later when she prepared supper, she mulled over the thought. Chili peppers. He always said chili peppers upset his belly. Maybe he could stand to suffer once in a while like she suffered. She pulled out the ingredients to make oven-baked barbeque pork with potato salad and baked beans. A little chili pepper would improve the taste of his favorite meal. It wouldn't take much.

As usual, Lillian arrived first and started to ready the place for the meeting. When she picked up a fallen limb and moved it to a pile behind a nearby tree, she found a wadded-up paper under the leaves. She straightened it and read.

"Mikie, I've tried to talk to you, but you won't listen. I've read that one of the biggest causes of marital problems is lack of communication. Well, we have plenty of lack in our communication. As a last resort, I'm writing you this letter, hoping you will at least read it and respond.

I've always loved you, but that love is quickly dying. In fact, there's very little left. We married young and we share too many memories to throw the love we've shared away, but that's exactly what you're doing. I am willing to forgive and get past your failure to be a husband to me if you are willing to change and be faithful to me. I can't take much more, and I won't.

I know you've had other affairs besides the one you're having now, but I am willing to forgive and move on if you will pledge your love to me again and agree to renew our vows. However, if you won't make this change, we're through. I will tell you one thing—if you refuse to stop your stupid affairs and running around on me, you will lose everything. And I mean everything—your home, your kids, your reputation, your bank account, and possibly your job. You'll be ruined. I've thought of a way to end everything for all of us if you continue to see her."

The letter had no signature, but something about the handwriting looked familiar.

She looked around but saw no one. The dirty paper had been there a while. Probably carried here by the wind from someone's trash or thrown from a passing vehicle. She didn't know who owned the property, and no houses were nearby. It was odd to find a letter out here in the woods.

"Whatcha got there?" Bella set her picnic basket on a log and spread out her blanket.

"It's a letter. I found it in the leaves over there." Lillian pointed and handed the letter to Bella. "It's a doozy, and whoever wrote it sounds fed up."

Bella read it with wide eyes. "Wow! You found it here? Wonder who wrote it?"

Kora arrived and read the letter. "Cool! We get to solve a mystery." She looked around. "Wonder what she has in mind? Sounds threatening to say the least." She sucked in her breath. "This letter might be evidence if a murder happens to someone named Mikie."

"But who wrote it?" Bella said. "We need to find out some way."

Lillian shrugged. "How can we possibly find out? There's no clue."

"We can keep our eyes and ears open. It's gotta be someone from around here. We might hear something."

Kora sniffed. "Humpf! I'm never anywhere to hear anything except at church. Even then, I can't talk to anyone." Lillian nodded in agreement. "Bella, you'll have to be our eyes and ears since Lillian and I are homebound."

Bella nodded. "I'll do it. I'll be a sleuth and use my nose to sniff around. I don't know Mikie, but maybe I'll overhear someone talking about a Mikie at Walmart or Sams. Or at the Dollar store. As small as this town is, I might hear something."

Lillian stuffed the letter into her pocket and pulled out her journal. "Have you ladies written anything interesting this week?"

"I wrote something, but it isn't interesting," Bella said.

Kora pulled out her blue and pink striped book. "Mine may be a little interesting, but I'm not sure. Here, I'll read it."

Dear Journal: While cleaning under the bed, I found a small gemstone. I think it's a ruby. I thought maybe it fell out of a piece of my jewelry, but I don't have any jewelry with stones like that. I found one on the internet that looks just like it, and it's worth a lot of money. I'm so excited. I wonder where it came from. When I get a chance, I'll take it to a jeweler and have it appraised. Maybe the jeweler will buy it from me. Maybe I'll end up rich.

Lillian laughed. "That's good, Kora. Nathan will have a hard time not letting you know he read your journal." She turned to Bella. "We want to hear your uninteresting entry, Bella."

Bella shrugged. "Y'all know Levi doesn't care what I write about. He won't read it anyway, so I just write for myself." She opened her journal and read.

Dear Journal: Today, I looked into the mirror, and an unhappy person looked back at me. Who is that woman in the mirror? I don't like her hair. I don't like her face. I don't like her figure. She's fat. She's sloppy. She's dumb. No, wait a minute! I am NOT dumb. I may be made to feel dumb sometimes, but I know I'm not. I looked at the person again. I think I need a new haircut, but I'm not ugly. I could stand to lose a little weight, but I'm not fat. I'm not a bad person. I can fix myself up a little better. Wear a little makeup. Get a new hairstyle. Dress a little neater. I can do this! Mirror, expect a new woman from now on.

"Bella!" Kora exclaimed. "You are a beautiful person. I hope Levi knows that."

"No, he doesn't," Bella said. "He always points out my faults and failures." She mimicked his voice. "You don't keep the house clean enough. It wouldn't hurt if you'd lose a little weight. You're so clumsy. Your voice is weird."

"I hate that our husbands don't see our value," Lillian said. "It's hard to see our own worth when they devalue us. Bella, you are a beautiful person. If you feel you need to improve some areas, then do that. But not because of him. Do it for yourself." She opened her journal. "My mind has been running along the same lines. Here's what I wrote Monday."

She read.

Dear Journal: So often, we think a person's value is in the eyes of another, but that isn't true. What someone else thinks of me is important only when that person is important to me. How God sees me is much more relevant and important because He sees me through eyes of love.

God's attitude about love is so much different from ours. According to Him, love is kind, patient, protects, trusts, hopes, rejoices in the truth, and doesn't give up. It does not dishonor others, does not envy or boast, is not self-seeking, is not easily angered, and does not keep a record of wrongs. So often, others love only when love is given. We sometimes love only when we get love or something else in return. I'm so glad God's love is unconditional. He loves me just because I am his creation—his child. Now, that's true love.

She lifted her eyes and looked at the two other women. "I want to display that kind of love, but I don't know if I can."

They nodded and murmured their agreement.

"It's hard," said Kora, "when the one who's supposed to love you is mean to you."

Lillian nodded. "It is, that's for sure. But remember girls, we can't control the behaviors of our husbands, but we can control ours. That's our job. The sad thing is, God will talk to them, but He won't make them listen."

"Ugh!" Kora rolled her eyes. "I wish he would knock them in the head and make them. I get so tired of putting up with Nathan's narcissism every day. But I do understand that we all have a will, and God won't override it."

"Do you want to hear what Levi did this week?" Bella sniffed. "Sometimes I wonder if there's anything in that head of his."

Lillian and Kora waited expectantly as she relayed the story.

"He wanted to grill some pork chops, so I prepared them for him. He started the grill, but it didn't get hot enough fast enough. So, he gets a cup of gas and throws it on the grill. The fire followed the gas all the way back to him and climbed up his britches leg. He stomped and slapped it out. It's a wonder he didn't catch fire and burn up."

Kora gasped. "Did the pork chops get done?"

"A little past well done," Bella said. "We ate them anyway. That man can't wait on anything. When I make supper, he fills his plate and starts eating before I set it on the table. The rest of us have to fend for ourselves. I make the kids wait until we ask God to bless our food, but he won't wait for anything."

Kora laughed so hard she snorted, and Lillian snickered behind her hand.

"I may be wrong in how I prayed this week," said Bella, "but Levi has been such a grouch and messy as all get out. He leaves his dirty clothes on the floor, gets toothpaste all over the bathroom sink, and leaves dirty dishes and beer cans all over the living room. He's a slob, and his body odor is horrendous. I get tired of cleaning up after him. I tell him I work the same as he does, but it makes no difference. When he gets home, he sits in the recliner in front of the TV until bedtime while I do all the housework and tend to the kids."

"So," said Kora, "what did you pray?"

"Lord, either change him or kill him, and right now, I don't care which." Her head bobbed up and down. "And I meant it, too!"

Lillian and Kora nodded. "Maybe we all need to pray like that," Kora said.

EIGHTEEN

During the morning service the following Sunday, Lillian and Kora stood talking in the foyer while their husbands chatted with a group of men.

Lillian touched Kora's arm. "Looks like your prayer has been answered. I see that Nathan came with you today."

"Yeah," Kora said. "I'm thankful for that. I think."

Nathan kept glancing toward the two women and finally walked over to Kora. He looked at Lillian, then at Kora. "Want to introduce me to your friend?" he said.

"Sure. Nathan, this is Lillian. We've met since I've been coming here. Lillian, my husband, Nathan."

When Lillian smiled and spoke to him, he barely nodded to her. "Where is your seat?" he asked Kora.

She guided him to the pew she usually occupied, and they sat down.

"Wait here," he said. "I'll be right back."

She observed as he approached a group of men and started laughing and talking with them. Lillian stood next to Kora's pew and continued talking to her until Nathan and Thomas came down the aisle toward them. Thomas took Lillian's arm, and they sat down two rows in front of the younger couple.

"Looks like we have a visitor today," Thomas said. "Says his name is Nathan." He glanced back, then frowned at Lillian.

"You seemed pretty friendly with his wife. Do you know her?".

"Kora? Yes, she goes to church here. It's nice that you were friendly with her husband. He needs us to make him feel welcome since he's new."

He scowled and ignored her comment. "What were you talking about?"

Lillian looked toward the pulpit where the director stood. "Shhh. Church is starting."

"We'll continue this later," he hissed in her ear.

Thomas left as usual when the sermon started, and Nathan rose and followed him. Lillian glanced back at Kora, and five minutes later, they met in the bathroom.

"Looks like Nathan is learning from Thomas," Kora said. "Now he's mad because I talked to you. I thought I'd like him to come to church with me, but if he doesn't let me have friends, I may not like it."

"Give it a chance," Lillian said. "It can take time for him to come around. Maybe he'll listen to Pastor Bill and get his heart right with God. Then things will be different."

Kora groaned. "He won't if he doesn't stay to hear the sermons. Besides, he says he and God are on good terms. I don't want to lose all my friends because he won't let me talk to them."

"I know," Lillian said. "I had so many friends before I married Thomas, but now I have to avoid them. I'm sure they think I'm stuck up."

"That's a terrible thought. I hope they don't think that. Of course, Thomas seems like a good Christian to everyone who sees him. Too bad they don't know how he really is."

"I've had a few give me dirty looks, I think because they wanted him. Little do they know how blessed they are that he chose me instead of them."

Kora sighed. "How sad to know that's true." She tapped her finger on her chin. "I've been thinking," she said, "maybe things would be better for Nathan and me if we had a baby. What do you think?"

Lillian leaned against the counter and crossed her arms. "I don't know, Kora. That's a hard one. If you have a baby and things are better between you, that would be great. But if things don't improve, it will be harder for you and rough on a child. Yes, that's hard, and I don't have an answer."

"I'm praying about it. I don't want to bring a child into a bad relationship."

They grew quiet when a lady entered the bathroom. Lillian mouthed to Kora that she was leaving. They both returned to their pews for the rest of the service.

After the service, Nathan and Thomas were sweet and attentive to the ladies, smiling at parishioners and shaking hands with the pastor.

When Thomas pulled the truck onto the road toward home, he hissed at Lillian. "I saw you coming out of the bathroom with Nathan's wife. What were you talking about?"

Lillian frowned. "So, we were both in the bathroom. There can be more than one woman in there, Thomas. There are stalls, you know. Doesn't the men's bathroom have stalls? Do you go in there only one at a time?"

He slapped the steering wheel. "Don't change the subject. I'm not talking about men, Lillian, I'm talking about you. You were talking to her before church started. What were you two talking about?"

She patted him on the leg. "Uh, let's see. I said, 'How are you today?' And she said, 'I'm fine. And you?' And I said, 'I'm doing well. The weather has been beautiful this week.' And she said, 'It sure has.' And I said...."

"You're lying," he growled. "Don't lie to me, woman."

"Don't ask silly questions, Thomas. We were simply holding a polite conversation. It's called small talk. That's all. There's nothing wrong with that. I don't understand why you are so suspicious of me and don't want me to talk to anyone. I don't do that to you."

"That's different," he said.

"Oh, you mean you're a man and can do what you want, but I'm a woman and must do as you say? Even if that were an issue, why do you have a problem with me talking to another woman?"

"Shut up!" he thundered. "You need to read your Bible. It plainly says for a woman to submit to her husband. Why do you have trouble submitting to me? If you don't obey the Bible, you'll go to hell. I don't want you to go there. Can't you see I love you?"

"I do submit to you, Thomas. Submit doesn't mean obey. That's entirely a different thing."

"Seriously? It's the same thing. I don't know where you get your information, but you need to change your source."

Lillian released a huge sigh and looked out the side window until they arrived home. No, this didn't feel anything like love. What could she say? What could she do? She could be a good wife. She had no problem submitting to him. She also recognized verbal and emotional abuse. She sent up a silent prayer asking for patience and wisdom to allow God to do His work and then wrote in her journal.

Dear Journal: The craziest thing happened today. A deer ran across the field, and my dog Jack started chasing it. He chased it up the hill and into the woods. In no time, here he came with the deer behind him. That dog ran from that deer across the field. Then they turned, and Jack chased the deer back up the hill. Back and forth they ran, the dog chasing the deer, then the deer chasing the dog. I really enjoyed the show.

At least it was a two-sided game, unlike some games people play. A game is no fun when the deck is stacked.

NINETEEN

A s they drove home, Nathan cursed Kora for talking to Lillian. "I saw the two of you women talking before church. What were you talking about?"

"Nothing important," Kora said. "Just small talk. You know, about the weather and such."

"You'd better not be talking to her about me."

"Nathan, I just like to talk to the other ladies. I want to have friends just like you do. You were talking to her husband, Thomas."

"That's different," he muttered.

"Can we invite them for lunch some Sunday?" she asked.

"No. Absolutely not. I don't want anyone to come over for anything. And that's final. We won't discuss it again."

She stared out the window a few moments, and then turned to him. "Nathan, why are you doing this? You weren't possessive like this when we first married. Now you act like I'm a terrible person and will do something wrong if you don't keep an eye on me."

His head whipped around, and he stared at her. "You think I'm possessive?"

"Yes. Aren't you?"

"No, of course not. I'm just concerned, that's all. I love you so much that I want you all to myself. Is there anything wrong with that?"

"I'm sorry, but it doesn't feel like love when you won't let me have friends or a job I love. I can love more than one person and one thing at a time. My love for you is different, though. I hold my love for you above all my love for everyone and everything except God. Can't you see that?"

"That's enough," he yelled. "I don't want to hear about all the things you supposedly love, and I don't want to hear anything else about you working. The Bible says for you to submit to your husband. That's all, Kora. Not another word."

"When do you ever read the Bible? Today's the first time you've attended church since we married. And you didn't even stay to hear the sermon."

"Oh, so you're better than me because you listen to the preacher? Shoot, I probably know as much about the Bible as he does. My mama used to read it to me every night."

Kora sighed. "I'm sure Pastor Bill reads and studies the Bible a lot. I like to hear him preach. He seems very knowledgeable and knows how to make his sermons interesting. I think you'd like to hear him preach."

Nathan snorted. "Humpf! I'll bet he doesn't know more than my mama."

Kora looked sideways at him. In a barely audible voice, she said, "Maybe you didn't listen to her enough."

She felt the air suck out of the vehicle when he drew in his breath. His face reddened, and then he turned white around the mouth. She stiffened, expecting an onslaught of venom from his mouth. And it came. He cursed and beat the steering wheel the rest of the way home until her ears burned. She hoped he wouldn't break the steering wheel, causing them to end up in the ditch.

When they arrived, she jumped out of the truck and ran into the house. She flipped off the crockpot, set a plate beside it, and disappeared into the spare bedroom, where she stayed the rest of the day. She would not listen to another vile word from his mouth, and if he didn't want another word from her, he wouldn't get one.

Later, when the back door slammed, she supposed he'd gone to the shop and would not return for a while. She slipped to her knees beside the bed and cried out to God. "Lord, please help me," she prayed. "I feel like a prisoner in my own home. I don't know what to do. I don't want to spend the rest of my life like this." She sobbed into a pillow, then shook herself. She had to stop this. She would not be a victim. She opened the door and looked out but didn't see him. She went into her bedroom, picked up her journal, and then returned to the spare bedroom. She lay on the bed and wrote, pouring her feelings onto the paper. Why should she care if he read it?

Dear Journal: Today has been a hard day for me. I feel lonely and sad, trapped in this house with nothing of my own. I must be the ugliest, most disagreeable person alive. What has made me so bad? What have I done wrong? I don't know. I'm tired. Tired of feeling alone. Tired of being so unattractive. Tired of living. Dear God, how can I change? What can I do to make my life better? Won't you help me?

"Kora!" Nathan had come back into the house, probably hungry. Should she answer him? She recalled Lillian's words. 'We can't make them do what is right, but we make sure we always do the right thing. We can't control other people's behaviors, but we can control our own.' She closed the journal and laid it on the chest beside the bed.

"I'm coming," she called. Glancing into the mirror, she straightened her hair, brushed the wrinkles out of her skirt, and walked out. Nathan stood in the kitchen drying his hands.

"I'm hungry," he said. "Do we have any meatloaf leftovers from yesterday?"

"Sure. Want a meatloaf sandwich with lettuce and tomato?"

"Umm, that sounds good. I'll pour some tea and get the

plates." He filled two glasses with ice and poured the tea. He set two plates on the table, then sat as she prepared the sandwiches. "Sweetheart," he said, "I'm sorry about being so harsh. But you shouldn't have said that about me not listening to my mom."

"No, I shouldn't have said that. I'm sorry."

"You do know I love you, right?"

She shrugged. How could she admit to his proclamation of love when she felt anything but love from him? Without turning, she sliced a tomato. Soon, his warm hands surrounded her. He pulled her close and kissed the back of her neck.

"I don't want you to be unhappy. Please, sweetheart, look at me." He turned her around to face him and lifted her chin with a finger. When she looked up, he kissed her. His gentleness made her cry. That's the way he used to be. What happened? What changed him?

He pulled her close and held her, stroking her hair. "I'm sorry, baby. I'm sorry I hurt you. I'm sorry I made you feel so bad."

"Oh, Nathan." She sobbed. "You scare me sometimes. Why do you do that? You know I can't stand to be yelled at."

He pushed her back and peered into her face. "Kora, I don't mean to scare you. I want our marriage to be strong and good. It's my job to provide for you. Do you think I can't do that? Is it not enough that I work to provide a good living for us? My mom had to work all the time after she and Dad divorced. I saw the negative affects it had on her. I don't want us to end up divorced. Do you want that?"

She stared at him. "No, of course not. But we are not your parents. Besides, I like to work. It's challenging for me. You know I always like to be challenged. And why do you think it's only your place to provide for us? If I work, we'll be able to pay our mortgage faster and have more things. Don't you want more things?"

He shook his head. "Nothing I can't pay for. The Bible says that women are to marry, have children, and manage the home. You can't do that if you work all day."

"The woman in Proverbs 31 worked to help provide for her family. Should we ever have any, I would never put a job before the house or children, or you, for that matter."

"The subject isn't up for discussion, Kora." His tone changed to rough and angry. "That's how I believe, and that's how it will be. I'm the head of this house, and we'll do what I say."

"But Nathan! We should be able to discuss everything. I should have a say in what goes on in our home and our marriage. I have a mind and an opinion. I'm equal with you."

He shoved her, and she fell into a chair. "I said end of discussion." He stalked out the door, and she sobbed into her hands. What had happened to her sweet husband?

She returned to the bedroom and started writing again.

Dear Journal: I'm back. What have I done to make my husband distrust me? What can I do to win back his trust? I want our marriage to be strong and happy. I feel like everything I do is wrong. I just don't know what to do anymore. When we first married, I thought nothing could make me happier. I was over the moon in love. What happened? How can I regain that happiness? How can it be wrong for me to have friends? Or a job? I believe God wants us to work together as a couple to better ourselves. It would be so great if we could support each other and do things together. How can that be wrong?

Maybe he needs to read this. Maybe it will open his eyes.

TWENTY

On Monday, the meteorologist forecasted rain for Wednesday, so Lillian texted Kora and Bella. "Sorry, girls, but while it's raining Wednesday, I'd like to pretend-plan a vacation somewhere, but I can't decide where. I thought about the Grand Canyon, but it may be too far. What do you think? Please delete this as soon as you read it. I'll do the same."

Then she opened her journal and wrote.

Dear Journal: I enjoyed the trip to Eureka Springs my hubby took me on. Now I want to go to more places. I want to spend a week at the beach, swimming in the warm waters of the Gulf of Mexico or the Atlantic Ocean. I'd like to visit the Smoky Mountains and walk the Appalachian trail. I want to see the giant redwood and sequoia trees in California and watch the crashing waves in the Pacific Ocean. God created such beauty in the world, and sometimes, I wish I were a bird so I could fly around the world to see the beauty of His creation. Wouldn't that be grand? But I know I can't be a bird—God created me as a human. I also know that everyone can't see the world. Many people never get to see past their own home or hometown. I'm thankful I can go places and do things, even though I'm limited.

She closed the journal and started a load of laundry when

she received a message from Bella and immediately one from Kora. Bella suggested Houston, and Kora thought Washington, D.C., would be best. Lillian grunted. They were no help at all. She shot back messages to each of them, then deleted the messages. Houston it is.

Lillian enjoyed the walk to Bella's house. Except for a short space where she had to walk along the highway, she could take a path through the woods that lined the narrow blacktop. She didn't mind the sprinkling rain. The light raincoat and rainboots she wore kept her from getting soaked from walking through the wet woods. The smell of wet leaf mold reminded her of playing in the woods as a child after a big rain. She walked faster, realizing it might be pouring when she started back. She would have to leave early enough to dry off and start supper before Thomas arrived home.

Bella's little white cottage sat in the middle of a pecan grove on the outskirts of the small rural town. Rain dripped off the maple trees and off yellow and white daisies that grew beside the walk up to the house. A calico cat snoozed in a rocking chair on the front porch. A red barn in the back housed a red tractor and other equipment.

She stepped onto the porch where Bella stood, water dripping from her hair. "I've locked myself out of the house," Bella said. "I went all around to see if maybe I had left a window open, but the only one maybe not locked is in the bathroom. It's so high I can't reach it.

"Oh, dear." Lillian glanced around. She looked at the rocking chair. "Can we use this chair to get to the window?"

Bella grimaced. "We can, but it won't be stable. Maybe you can hold it while I climb up."

They dragged the chair around the house to the high bathroom window. Lillian held onto the rocker while Bella climbed up. She pushed up the unlocked window. It was small, but she thought she could climb through.

She looked down at the white top she wore. "I don't want to stain my white shirt," she said. "Think it'll be okay if I pull it off?"

Lillian looked around. "Since you don't have close neighbors on this side, I'm sure it'll be okay."

Bella shed the shirt and threw it through the window.

"I hope you can get through," Lillian said, "because if you can't, you'll be out here wearing only your bra."

"Yeah," said Bella. "My hooter-holders are a little skimpy to wear around the neighborhood in broad daylight."

"Hooter-holders?" Lillian laughed. "At least your hooter-holders cover you pretty well."

"Hold on. I'm going in." Bella pulled herself over the windowsill and through the open window. About halfway through, she started struggling. Lillian ducked to keep from being kicked in the head.

"What's wrong?" Lillian tried to push her up.

"I'm stuck," Bella said. "And I'm afraid I'll fall and hurt myself. I'm over the commode, and the floor is kinda far down."

"Oh, dear, I don't want you to get hurt."

"I don't want to break the commode."

Lillian pushed and huffed. "Maybe you can hold on to the commode and lower yourself down."

"First, I have to get my big butt through this window." Bella strained and wiggled until she managed to get in.

Lillian heard a crash, a flush, and a groan. "Are you okay?" she yelled.

"Yes, I'm all right. I just broke a lamp."

"Better than breaking your head or arm," Lillian said. "Are you able to go unlock the front door?"

"Yes, I think so." Bella moaned. "I'll meet you there."

Lillian ran around the house and almost collided with a couple standing by the porch holding a red striped umbrella.

"Hello," she said. "Are you Bella's neighbors?"

"Yes," the man answered. "We live over there." He pointed to a house across the street. "Is Bella okay? Looks like she may have run into some trouble."

Lillian bit her lip. "Yes, she's fine. She locked herself out and had to crawl through a window."

The lady held her hand over her mouth, and her eyes twinkled. The man looked at his wife and chuckled. "Well, have a nice day," he said. "And tell Bella we hope she didn't hurt anything crawling through that window."

"Yes," the wife said. "We're glad she wasn't left hanging."

"Please tell her she has plenty of support." Their laughter rose as their legs under the umbrella moved on down the street.

"Come in out of the rain." Bella said as she opened the door. "Give me your raincoat. I'll hang it up to drip. Put your boots over there." She pointed to a rug beside the door.

"Let me take care of these wet things while you dry off," Lillian said.

"Okay. Kora is on the way. She doesn't have as far to walk as you, but it's still a little jog from her farm. She called and said she's bringing a salad to go with my chicken strips."

Lillian pulled some cookies and crackers from her bag and helped herself to a glass of tea. Bella returned, drying her hair. "I hope this rain stops soon," she said. "I like rainy days when I can curl up with a snack and a book."

"Yes. A good book is better than crawling through the bathroom window."

Kora came in about that time and laughed as Bella relayed what had happened.

"But you don't know all of it," Lillian said. She told them about the couple she met in front of the house.

"Oh no!" Bella gasped. "You think they saw me in my hooter-holders?"

"Considering what they said, I'm sure they did." Lillian snickered while Bella covered her face with her hands.

"I don't know how I'll ever face them again," she groaned.

"Aw, I wouldn't worry," Kora said. "I'm sure they watch TV commercials that show more than you did."

Bella removed the chicken strips from the air fryer. "I'm glad you girls came in spite of the rain. It's like a breath of fresh air when we get together."

"Bet that fresh air hit you this morning." Kora giggled.

"Oh, hush." Bella waved a hand toward Kora. "I'll have a hard time living this one down."

Kora dipped her chicken strip in BBQ sauce. "Oh, we'll never let you live this down."

"I know one thing," Lillian said. "Friends may come and go, but boobs are always in front of you."

Bella spurted her drink all over the table. Kora grabbed napkins and cleaned up the mess. Laughter filled the kitchen, and the friends relationships deepened as they laughed together. They settled down to discuss the events of the week.

"I have an idea about our journals," Lillian said. "Let's make a change. Let's make them prayer journals."

Kora frowned. "You mean write prayers instead of stories?"

"Yes. At least some entries." Lillian pulled her journal out of her bag. "Listen to this."

Father, I know you hear me because your Word says you do. It also says that if I know you hear me, then I know you answer me. I'm depending on that now. I need an attitude adjustment.

Sometimes, my attitude stinks, and I say and do things I shouldn't. Will you please help me? I want to have a good, positive attitude that honors you. Thank you, Jesus. Amen

Bella stared at Lillian. "You're saying your attitude is bad? What about Thomas? He's the rotten apple."

"Yeah," said Kora. "Thomas is the one needing an attitude adjustment."

"While that may be true," Lillian said, "I must pray for myself to change first. And I do have a bad attitude sometimes. My attitude is my problem, and until I get that right, I don't need to ask for anyone else to be fixed." She looked at the dejected faces before her. "I'm not telling y'all to pray that way. You pray how you feel and ask for what you want."

"I do often have a bad attitude," Bella said. "I know I need help in that area."

"Me, too," Kora agreed. "Sometimes I feel like the lowest of lows. Pastor Bill keeps saying we should always have a positive attitude. Every time he preaches on that subject, I get convicted. I know I need to change."

"We'll pray for each other," Lillian said. "We all need to change in some areas."

"Y'all need to pray for me this week," Bella said. "We're going to have dinner with Levi's family. I love them, and they treat me like a daughter."

"Then what's the problem?" asked Kora.

"The problem is Levi. He never wants to visit my family and acts like a jerk when he does. He sits sulking in a corner and never wants to stay long. He barely talks to anyone. But when we go to see his family, he's all smiles and a regular jabber bird, and we stay a long time." She hesitated. "I guess I'm the problem. I resent the way he acts with my family. See? There's my bad attitude."

Kora frowned. "At least you can see your family. I can't even see mine."

"Yeah," agreed Lillian. "If it weren't for my telephone, I'd be a stranger to my own kids."

"I think one day I'll borrow a car and go see my parents," Kora said. "I really miss them."

"You can borrow mine," Bella offered. "I'm home Tuesdays and Fridays."

"I just may do that," Kora said.

Martha Rodriguez

TWENTY-ONE

*L*illian left the meeting early enough to dry off before Thomas came home from work, but the rain increased before she'd walked half mile down the road. The light raincoat didn't keep her dry, and the wind made it impossible to use the umbrella. Rain pelted her head, causing water to run down her face, burning her eyes with running mascara until she could hardly see. She stumbled over a log, almost falling into a wide puddle as she plodded through soggy leaves on the woodsy path. Walking along the highway would be easier, but she didn't want to be on the road for someone to see her and offer her a ride.

She usually loved the smell of rain, but the musty scent of wet leaves and the cold that crept through her shoes and up her pant legs chilled her and hampered her speed. She could taste hairspray as water from her hair ran into her mouth. Would she make it in time to dry her hair and put on dry clothes? If she didn't, what excuse could she use? She did her best not to lie when Thomas questioned her. She wanted him to be able to trust her.

Just as she entered the backyard, a force hit her from behind, and she fell face-first into the muddy yard. She lay still a moment. What hit her? The rain pattered on the leaves by her head might have lulled her to sleep if she were dry and in her warm bed. She pulled herself up to her knees. A big, black Billy goat stood with head lowered, staring into her eyes,.

"Billy Bob, what are you doing out here? How'd you get out of the pen?" He shook his head and his tail wagged viciously. "It's me, fella. Don't you know who I am? Don't you dare butt me again."

She rose and petted his head. "Come on. Let's get you to the barn." He followed her through the gate and ran to join the other goats. She hurried into the house to shower and start supper. She threw her wet clothes into the washing machine and went into the kitchen. At least now she had a reason to be wet when Thomas came home.

Thomas came in with a big smile and hugged her hard. "I've missed you today, sweetheart," he said. "Why are you wet? Have you been in the rain?"

She explained about the wayward goat, and he hugged her hard. He sniffed her hair. "I like that shampoo you use. You smell good. I've missed you."

"Really? Why have you missed me today?"

He ignored her question as he picked up the lid from a pot and sniffed the contents. "Umm. That smells wonderful. Supper about ready?"

"Yes. It will be on the table by the time you're washed up." She reached up for a kiss, and he obliged. At first a little peck, then he pulled her into a tight embrace and kissed her with passion.

"No wonder I missed you so much," he said. "You feel good and smell wonderful. Supper may have to wait."

She laughed and patted him on the butt. "You go wash, and we can continue this later."

He yelled at her from the bathroom. "I think we have some cats living in the barn. Know anything about that?"

She yelled back. "Really? Are they cute? Did you feed them?"

"I don't know about cute, but they look pretty healthy. A black and white mama with a gray-colored baby. No, I didn't feed them, but you might want to put out some leftovers or something for them later. Wouldn't want them to starve, right?"

She giggled. "That might be a good idea," she yelled.

He came down the hall, rubbing his face with a towel. "That's what I thought. Poor little creatures. Maybe they'll keep the mice away. We'll need to have them fixed, or we'll end up with a barn full of cats."

"That's true," she said.

"We hired a new guy for the road crew today." Thomas put a spoonful of potatoes on his plate. "I'm a little leery of him, though. Bob recommended him. Looks like he hasn't done much work anywhere since he graduated high school three years ago."

"Bob is your road foreman, right?"

"Yes. I think the guy is kin to him somehow."

"It might not be a good idea for him to recommend a family member."

"It usually isn't. If the guy doesn't work out, it looks bad on the one who recommended him. I'm concerned about Bob anyway. I've been getting complaints about him."

He continued to chat about work, and they laughed at a joke one of his co-workers told him. After supper, he popped in and out of the kitchen to talk to her. Even though he didn't offer to help with the chores, she enjoyed his attention. When she finished and turned off the kitchen lights, he sat in his recliner and pulled her into his lap. At first, she stiffened, but he stroked her back, and soon she relaxed in his arms.

"I'm glad I married you," he said. "You're such a beautiful woman and a good person."

She pulled back and looked him in the face. "Really? You think I'm beautiful? Even with this graying hair and these wrinkles?"

He stroked her hair and then her face. "I love your salt and pepper hair, and you don't have wrinkles. I see women your age who have a lot of wrinkles. Your skin is smooth and silky." He pulled her close and squeezed her.

"Thank you for saying that." She caressed his face. "You are a handsome man. When I married you, I became the envy of a lot of women. Some of them told me so, and others just gave me looks that said it."

He laughed, and she laid her head on his shoulder, enjoying the love he expressed. Maybe he would treat her like this from now on. What a wonderful thought! He pushed her into the floor, then laughed, stood, and picked her up. She giggled as he carried her into the bedroom where she experienced more love than she had since they married.

TWENTY-TWO

"Bella, when will you be ready to go? My family is expecting us at 5:30 for supper." Levi stomped into the kitchen, threw his jacket into a corner, and pulled a can of beer from the refrigerator.

Bella filled her cheeks with air, and then blew it out. "I know. I'm trying to hurry. Did you get the deviled eggs made?"

"Yep. They're all done, and I gotta say they look pretty good. Maybe even perfect." He opened the refrigerator and pulled out a platter of eggs covered with plastic wrap.

"Beautiful." Bella smiled and nodded. "You did great, sweetheart. Thank you so much for doing those."

He kissed her forehead. "It's the least I could do since you had to work today."

Bella put a dish of food into a carrier and covered it with a towel. "Addison," she yelled. "Trevor! Come on, kids, we have to go."

They loaded the food into the SUV and soon carried it into Levi's parents' home.

Bella loved Levi's mom and stepdad. Since she had married into the family eighteen years before, they had been welcoming and supportive, making her feel a part of the family.

"You'll be proud of your son," Bella told Levi's mom, Judy. "He made the deviled eggs all by himself." She handed Judy the platter while Levi stood grinning.

"May I taste one?" Judy peeled back the plastic. "They sure do look good. You did a great job." She stuffed an egg into her mouth, and her eyes grew wide. She chewed and swallowed with some difficulty. "Ummm. They're good."

Bella frowned. Judy scrunched up her nose and raised her eyebrows. Bella took an egg and stuffed it into her mouth. She retched and spat it into the trash can. She looked closely at the egg platter and then at Levi, who stood with an open mouth.

"Levi, how did you make these eggs?"

"Just like you told me." He held up his fingers as he repeated her instructions. "First, I boiled the eggs, peeled them, and cut them in half. Then I mixed mayonnaise and mustard in a bowl. I added some salt and pepper. Then, I put the mixture into the boiled egg whites. I made it swirly just like you said."

"What did you do with the egg yolks?"

"I threw them out. You didn't say anything about using them."

Bella and Judy hooted while Levi stood looking sheepish.

"What did I do wrong?" he asked.

When Bella finally contained her laughter, she explained that he should have mixed the mayonnaise and mustard mixture with the egg yolks. During dinner, Judy told everyone about the deviled eggs.

"Y'all will never let me live this down," Levi said. Bella assured him they wouldn't. She couldn't wait to tell Lillian and Kora.

While they enjoyed the meal without deviled eggs, Levi's

dad, Ray, told stories of Levi's childhood.

"After he turned fifteen," Ray said, "he wanted to know what would happen to the hogs we raised. He had a fit when I told him they would be butchered. He had no idea ham and bacon came from hogs. I don't know what I did wrong in raising him. Guess I failed to teach him about living on a farm."

Trevor giggled at the thought of his dad being ignorant about hogs. "Dad, I can't believe you didn't know where ham comes from. Even I know that."

Levi laughed and rubbed his son's head. "I taught you that, son, so you wouldn't be ignorant like me."

"There are still some things Dad doesn't know," said Addie. "Like how to empty the trash can and do laundry."

Levi's face reddened and he leaned toward Addie. "Little girl, I expect your mama to teach you how to do those things so I don't have to."

"Son, it wouldn't hurt you to do laundry and dishes once in a while," Judy said.

"Is this pick-on-Levi night?" Levi said. "Enough with the stories. Dad, we need to talk about that new tractor you're looking to buy. Is it a Farmall? When we finish eating, I want you to take me to see it."

While the men talked about farm equipment, Bella and Judy cleared the table and cleaned the kitchen.

"Is everything all right, Bella? I know Levi is rough in some ways, but he's a good man. Is he treating you and the kids good?"

Bella looked at Judy a moment before she answered. "He is a little rough sometimes. But he works hard to make a good living for us. It helps that I work only a couple of days a week, because he doesn't help at all with the housework. He does keep the outside looking good, though. That's important, and

I know it's hard work."

"I hope he's good to the kids. His dad wasn't a good man. He treated Levi awful."

Bella turned to put away a dish. "I hate that for him. I know it made his life hard. Seems like, though, that a man mistreated by a parent would be determined to treat his own children good. Doesn't it?"

"You'd think so. But often it goes the other direction. I just want my son to treat my grandchildren good."

"He's cranky with them, but he's never been abusive to them. He'd better not, either. I won't put up with that. I won't stand by and have my kids mistreated."

Judy grimaced. "No, you can't. If he mistreats them, you tell me, and together we'll set him straight."

Bella laughed. "I'll do that. Between the two of us, maybe we can keep him in line."

Later, Bella wrote in her journal.

Dear Journal: I do love my mother-in-law. She's been so good to me. I can see a little of her in Levi, but he must take more after his biological dad. His stepdad is loving and sweet to his wife. He is neat and helps her with the housework. I sure wish Levi were more like that. I had fun tonight, though. I loved the stories about his childhood. Some I've heard before, but Roy gets such a kick out of telling them, I love hearing them again.

Dear Lord, please show me how to be a better wife to my husband. I need a better attitude. I know I'm not perfect. I'm sure there are things about me he can't stand. I want to be the kind of wife he needs and the kind of mom my kids need. I know you hear me, so thank you. Amen.

TWENTY-THREE

*L*illian hummed as she peeled potatoes and fried pork chops. The last few days had been wonderful. Thomas had been loving and attentive, and she basked in his love every evening. Her feelings of romance escalated when one evening he helped her clean the kitchen and put in a couple of loads of laundry.

But it came to an end. She felt her heart would break.

He returned home from work one day in a dark mood. She met him at the door as she had been doing. His face wore clouds and his shoulders stooped. She raised her face to kiss him, and he barely gave her a peck. He pushed her hand aside when she reached to caress his face. Immediately, she drew back.

"Is something wrong, sweetie?" she asked.

"No, of course not." His harsh tone pushed her further away. "Why do you always think something is wrong with me? I don't feel in the mood for your sweet talk." She turned to tend to the cooking food, and he pushed past her. He clicked on the TV and went into the bathroom. When he returned, he slumped into his recliner. "Food ready yet?" he yelled.

"Almost." She finished the meal and called him in to eat. He skipped the blessing over the food, and they ate in silence. He quietly watched TV, speaking only to ask her for a bowl of ice cream. She wondered if something had happened at work but dared not ask. Was it too much to dream of a time when they could sit together and talk about everyday things? About their feelings like best friends do? Like she and Jim did. No, she couldn't allow herself to think about Jim. Besides being unfair to Thomas, it made her miss him more.

While he brooded in front of the TV, she read for a while and then pulled out her journal and started to write.

"What's that stuff you're always writing?" he asked.

"This? It's my journal. I like to write. This is one way I can spend time while you're watching TV."

He frowned. "What do you write about?"

"Want to read it?" She closed the journal and held it out. His brows knitted and he shook his head. She stifled a sigh of relief and picked up her pen.

"Why don't you write a book? Then you could get paid and make it worthwhile instead of a waste of time."

"Hum—I never thought of that. Maybe I should. Do you really think I could?"

He nodded. "Sure. You're creative enough and smart enough. You might become rich and famous."

She laughed. "Oh, Thomas, you're not serious. I know nothing about writing a book. I just write things I think about and dream about."

"Maybe I do need to read what you've written."

She tensed. But what could it hurt? She held it out to him, and again, he refused it. "I have considered trying to create a children's book. Of course, I wouldn't know what to do with it if I did. I couldn't illustrate it."

"I'll bet you could if you tried. Aren't children's book

illustrations pretty simple?"

"Some are, but some are elaborate and beautiful."

"Well, do what you want. I don't care anyway."

She frowned and shook her head. "For a moment, you sounded like you cared what I do. That was nice while it lasted."

He scowled. "Oh really? You think I don't care?"

She flipped her hand toward him. "Sometimes, I guess you do. Sometimes I feel like you don't."

He straightened. "Lillian, if I didn't care about you, why did I marry you? Of course, I care about you." He grinned. "You write a book and get famous, and then I'll really care."

Is he serious? Or just playing? How could she tell the difference? "Thomas, what would you do if I became rich and famous?"

His scowl returned. "I'd have to lock you up to keep you away from all the men who would want a part of you." He slumped into his recliner. "Just don't count on becoming rich or famous. Then we won't have to worry about it."

He turned to the TV and sat pouting, so she picked up her notebook.

Dear Journal: They say that all good things must come to an end. I refuse to believe that. I think all good things may come at a price, but they don't have to come to an end. At least, I hope not. The best things in life are free in one sense but pricy in another. It's all in what's important to us. I didn't realize how important my friends were until I lost them. I found out that I appreciated my loved ones more after I lost them than I did while I still had them. How sad.

Sitting here with the TV running hour after hour is a waste of time. Yes, we need some downtime. Time to unwind. Time to slough off all the stress and aggravation of the day. But it's easy to spend countless hours being entertained and do nothing worthwhile, just like I'm doing right now. Guess I should get ready for bed.

Father, time is valuable, and I don't want to waste it. Please give me wisdom to use the time You give me to better myself or to benefit someone. Thank You for giving me time.

Thomas remained withdrawn when they went to bed, and she remained silent. The next morning, he ate the food she prepared and left without a word. She packed a sack lunch and headed for the *lieu de rencontre*. She looked forward to visiting with the girls after such a quiet spell at home, but she hesitated. Should she stay at home today? No, she would meet with her friends. She looked forward to seeing them each week.

TWENTY-FOUR

*W*hen she arrived at the clearing in the woods, Kora sat in the middle of her quilt crying.

Lillian rushed to her side. "What's wrong, sweetie?"

Kora shook her head and swiped at her nose with a tissue. "I messed up, Lillian." Sobs shook her body. Bella arrived and ran to her.

"What happened?" Bella asked. "How did you mess up?"

Kora drew in a sharp breath and exhaled. "I wanted to get back at Nathan for how he treats me. I thought I could be as mean as he is, but I can't. I don't want to. I burned his bread and dumped salt on his potatoes. Right on his plate. I ruined his meal. He knew I did it on purpose." She sniffed. "You know what he said? He said he thought I loved him. He told me it isn't like me to be spiteful." Her eyes widened. "And he's right. It isn't like me to be spiteful. I know I lost some or maybe all of his respect for me." She sobbed. "Know what I think? I think he doesn't even know he's mean to me. He always tells me he loves me and doesn't want me to do wrong things and go to hell." Another sob came from deep within her chest. "I really hurt his feelings."

"Oh, Kora." Lillian pushed Kora's hair back from her wet face. "I hate that for you. Our men don't seem to understand how they hurt us. I've thought about doing something to get even with Thomas, but I thought better of it. You know what they say—two wrongs don't make a right."

Kora leaned her head on Lillian's shoulder and wept while Bella rubbed her back until she finished her cry. She mopped her face and then looked toward Lillian's basket.

"What'd you bring to eat?" she asked.

Bella laughed. "Now you're hungry, huh? I am, too. Let's eat."

They enjoyed chicken salad sandwiches and iced sweet tea as they caught up on their week. A squirrel came over to investigate, and Bella rewarded him with a pecan from her salad.

"I have a journal entry," Bella said. "It isn't anything special, though."

"Okay," Lillian said. "I'll bet it will be special."

Bella read.

Dear Journal: Today, I made Addison an outfit for her school Sweetheart Dance. She has grown up so fast into a beautiful young woman. I don't know for sure, but I think she has a boyfriend. I've tried to teach her to be respectful, but maybe I've failed to be an example. It's hard sometimes when I don't feel like I'm treated with respect as a woman. I want her to learn how to be a lady and demand to be treated like one. I don't want to see her hurt. I want her to choose carefully who she dates so she won't end up married to the wrong person.

Lillian nodded, and Kora sighed. "Yeah—like we did," Kora said. They sat in silence for a few minutes, and Kora let out another long sigh.

"Why the big sigh?" asked Lillian.

"Nathan has this new thing he does that drives me crazy."

Kora put her hand to her forehead. "He sits in front of the TV with the remote and switches the channels constantly. He watches a documentary for about a minute, then changes it to a Western. Three minutes later, he switches it to a sitcom, which I enjoy. But before it ends, we're watching a crime show, then a different western. Then it's a show where greasy men with greasy hair and beards remodel old cars. In a few minutes, it's back to a cooking show — the western — the documentary. It's driving me berserk."

"Good grief!!" Lillian said. "That would drive anyone berserk. At least Thomas occasionally watches a good movie, as long as it isn't a Hallmark. He hates those."

"Oh," Bella said. "I love those movies, even though they are totally predictable. Levi likes old sitcoms and classic films. I'm glad he does because I do, too. Sometimes, while he's at work, I watch a Hallmark movie, especially at Christmas."

"Oh, what would we do without our men to keep us entertained." Kora picked up a leaf and spun it between her fingers. "Sometimes I think I would like to find out."

Lillian shook her head. "I understand how you feel. Sometimes I feel that way, too. But we can't allow ourselves to think like that. That would start us on a downhill slide that would be hard to stop."

Bella threw a leaf at Lillian. "How can you stay so positive all the time? Don't you ever want to knock Thomas in the head and say God did it?"

Lillian laughed. "Sure, I do. Just about every day. But I remember the vow I made before God to love, honor, and obey till death do us part."

Kora gasped, "You honestly promised to obey? Not me. I took that part out. I don't think anyone says that anymore."

Lillian grimaced. "Yeah, but Thomas insisted. Now I understand why. He knew I would take vows seriously."

"I take the till-death part seriously," Kora said. "Is it wrong to pray to be a widow?"

Lillian patted her hand. "Kora, I don't think you really want that. Wouldn't it be better to pray for our men to change?"

"Yeah," Kora said, "but how long will that take? How much abuse do we have to suffer waiting for them to change?"

"I don't know." Lillian groaned. "Lord, help us be patient."

"Oh, dear," Bella said. "Grandma always said that if you pray for patience, you get troubles. We don't need more troubles."

"We sure don't," Kora said. "But I do need patience. I'm lacking in that area."

They all agreed, and then Kora pulled out her journal. "That reminds me. I have been thinking that I need an attitude adjustment. Listen to this." She read from her journal.

Dear Journal: I'm so mad at myself. I'm trying to improve my attitude, but it's in the mud today. I woke up this morning feeling dejected and have continued feeling that way all day. I must get out of the pigsty!

So why am I dejected? Because I used a new recipe for supper last night, and it tasted awful. Seems like nothing I do anymore turns our right. Nathan hated it. I hated it! Why do I torture myself by trying new things? I should just continue doing the same things I've always done. But that gets so boring. I want to try new things, like I want to go to new places and see new things. I'm stuck in a rut. My life is going nowhere. Ugh!

"That's exactly how I feel," Bella said. "My life is going nowhere fast."

Lillian grabbed her bag. "Know what we all need right now? A chocolate bar." She handed the other two chocolate bars and opened one for herself.

"Oh, goodness," said Kora. "This is exactly what I need. It's perfect after my chicken sandwich." She rubbed her stomach and turned to Bella. "Say, did you ever find out who the Mikie in the letter is?"

"Not yet," Bella said. "I've been listening when I go anywhere. The other day, I followed two women through Walmart, and one said her friend got caught having an affair with some guy. But she never said his name."

"She never said anything about her friend getting murdered?" Kora asked.

"No, but she did say the woman's husband almost killed her. Nothing about the man's wife going after her."

"Guess we'll have to keep listening," Lillian said. "If some woman wants my husband, she can have him."

Kora threw an apple core toward a tree. "Here ya go, little squirrel." She turned to Lillian. "I saw Victoria making goo-goo eyes at Thomas Sunday. Maybe he'll run off with her then you won't have to worry about breaking a vow."

"He's threatened it," she said, "and she's warned me. I told him if that's what he wants, he has my permission. I'm leaving it up to God and him. That's one battle I choose not to fight."

Bella leaned forward. "You mean he threatened to run off with Victoria?"

Lillian hugged herself. "He did." She swallowed. "I think he knows what he'd have with her, but she doesn't have a clue what she'd get with him. Maybe they deserve each other."

"I'm sorry, Lillian," Kora said. "I know that hurts."

Lillian slumped against a tree. "It does, but I feel helpless. I try to be a good wife. I flirt with him and agree to just about anything he wants. I don't know what else to do."

"She is a big flirt," Kora said. "I've seen her flirt with about every man in church. No telling how she acts outside of church.

One Sunday, she batted those fake eyelashes at Lisa's hubby. I thought Lisa would take her down."

Bella laughed. "She'd be the one to do it. She's a hefty gal. I'd hate to tangle with her."

"She's fearless, too. Once, she stood up to old Ron Harris when he called her kids brats. She told him he needed to check out his own house rats before he commented on anyone else's pets." Kora slapped her leg. "He backed down quick. I about fell over laughing. You know what a hypocrite he is."

"What are you girls taking to the church dinner next Sunday?" Bella asked.

"I hate to take anything," Kora said. "I'm not a very good cook."

"I beg your pardon," Lillian said. "I ate some of the rice and chicken casserole you made last time. I loved it."

Kora smiled. "Well, I guess I can take that again. I got a lot of compliments for it. What are you taking, Lillian?"

Lillian broke a twig she held in her fingers. "Thomas always complained about me spending money on special ingredients to make anything. But not anymore. At the last dinner, I bought stuff to make an Ambrosia salad. You know, pineapples, marshmallows, cool whip, mandarin oranges, nuts, and maraschino cherries. He about took my head off for that. Then, when everyone at the dinner started bragging on it, I implied he came up with it. Right in front of him." She giggled. "So, the other day, he asked me what I will make and what he needs to buy. I know he'll take the credit for it. So, I'm looking for a recipe for something extravagant to make. A main dish and a dessert."

Bella and Kora giggled. "Oh, smart girl!" Kora said. "You're good at getting around him."

"Yeah," said Bella. "We need to take lessons from you."

"Well, I have been around the block a few times," Lillian said. "After all, this is not my first husband. Just the most exasperating one." She smiled, then her smile turned into a chuckle. "I remember once when Jim and I attended a church dinner, and he found a fly in his food. It just happened that the fly was in a meatball that the sweetest little lady at church had made. She sat beside him, and he couldn't figure out how to get rid of it without her seeing. He didn't want to hurt her feelings, so he ate that fly. I had to go to the bathroom and throw up." She sighed. "That's the kind of person he was. He wouldn't hurt anyone, especially me."

"Oh, Lillian," said Kora. "That's the sweetest story, even if it did make me gag. I know you miss him so much."

Another big sigh escaped from Lillian. "I do. But I must learn how to live the life I have now. It's inconvenient, but I own it since I chose it."

"I chose my life, but I don't own it." Bella buried her hands in her hair. "When we first married, I thought I couldn't have found anyone better. We did everything together and laughed all the time. He even went to church with me. He turned bad afterward."

"Mine, too," said Kora. "He changed, and that isn't fair. That's deceitful at best."

Lillian sat quietly, deep in thought. Finally, she spoke. "Ladies, it is what it is, I guess. What we have to consider is how God looks at our situations. I'm convinced that He sees things differently than we do. We are only responsible for our own actions and attitudes. And I know my attitude today is not what it should be." She rose and gathered her things. "I'm going home. I need to spend some time alone with the One who cares more about me than anyone else ever could."

Goodbyes were brief. They would see each other on the weekend, God willing.

TWENTY-FIVE

When she arrived home, Thomas sat on the porch.
"Where have you been?" he asked.
"I went for a walk," she said.

"What's in the basket?"

"My lunch. I had a picnic in the woods." She told the truth, so far.

She watched his face, expecting it to show anger. Except for a slight twitch at the outside corner of his left eye, his expression remained blank. He held out his hand, and she handed him the basket. He lifted the cloth and looked inside. Then he handed it back to her.

"You're home early," she said. "Are you okay?"

"I'm fine. Is supper ready?"

"It isn't time for supper. I'll start to work on it right away."

He patted the seat next to him. "You don't have to. Sit here by me."

She sat—stiffly at first, then leaned back and tried to relax. She didn't know what to expect from him.

"Did you have a good picnic by yourself or with someone else?"

"I had a nice time. Why are you home early?"

His face reddened. "It's nothing to you that I'm home

early. Can't I come to my own home any time of the day? "

"You questioned me about my day. I can only assume that's because you care about me like I care about you. I'm just concerned that something may be wrong. You don't usually take off early."

He frowned. "No, nothing is wrong. Things were slow at the office, so I took the afternoon off." He looked at her again. "Do you go on picnics often while I'm gone?"

"About once a week," she said. "I enjoy walking in the woods. I like to watch squirrels, rabbits, and birds. Sometimes, I see some deer. Occasionally, a fox. Those little creatures are so pretty and interesting. I'm thankful God created a beautiful world and allows us to live in it. I think that's special." She realized she was bordering on lying and didn't want to lie to her husband. She had to get his mind on something else.

"I've been looking for a good recipe for the church dinner on Saturday. I want to make something special."

He smiled. "Make me a list of what you need, and I'll pick it up after work tomorrow. You making a dessert?"

"Yes. I found a recipe for Italian Cream Cake that sounds good. And I'm looking at a recipe for orange chicken with rice."

He nodded. "I like Italian Cream Cake. My aunt used to make those." He stood. "Come on, and I'll help you with supper. I'm starting to feel hungry,"

Her eyes widened, and she jumped up. "I like that idea. My belly is feeling a little empty, too." She sent a silent 'Thank You' up to God.

Saturday, the church folks gathered in the fellowship hall

for a church dinner. Thomas proudly carried Lillian's casserole dish and smiled at everyone he met. Lillian followed behind with her Italian Cream Cake.

"What did you bring today, Thomas?" a lady asked.

"My special Orange Chicken with rice," he said. "It's a new recipe."

Lillian grinned. She'd made the dish, but he could take credit. No one had to know.

"Oh, that looks good." Pastor Bill said as Lillian set the cake on the dessert table and removed the cover from the rice dish.

His wife, Katie, set down a covered dish and gushed over the Orange Chicken. "Our Thomas is a good chef," she said. "His creations are attractive and delicious. And just smell that aroma!" She turned and spoke to those standing around. "Ladies, we're going to have to step up our game in the cooking department," she said. "Thomas is making us look bad."

Every woman in the room headed over to investigate his prize dish while he beamed. Lillian busied herself, uncovering dishes and setting out serving utensils. When she completed that job, she poured herself a drink and sat at a nearby table, watching. He thoroughly enjoyed all the attention until Victoria elbowed her way to the center of the group and stood beside him. Lillian noticed his expression. He scowled and pulled away from Victoria and then edged through the group, talking to different ladies. Victoria forced her way through them and stayed by his side.

Lillian was somewhat surprised that Victoria's attention seemed to annoy him. He acted like he wanted to get away from her. Time for an intervention. Lillian sidled over to him, smiling and speaking to everyone she met. When she reached Thomas's side, she wedged between him and Victoria and joined his conversation with an older lady. He turned and smiled at her and then put an arm around her shoulders and squeezed. Victoria rolled her eyes, snorted, and left.

Lillian turned to fill her glass when she noticed a lady sitting alone at a corner table. She sidled over to the lady and introduced herself. She recalled sitting alone so many times, wishing she had someone to talk to. The woman introduced herself as Marcy Owens, and they chatted for a while.

"I've seen you sitting toward the back," Lillian said, "but I've never spoken to you. Of course, Thomas is always in a hurry to leave, so I don't really talk to anyone."

Marcy nodded. "I've noticed that you don't talk much. But I remember that before you married Thomas, you talked to folks."

Lillian blushed. "I did. I miss that, too. Thomas doesn't like me talking to people."

Marcy lowered her voice. "Is he jealous of you?"

Lillian blinked but nodded. "Yes. I don't know why. I try to avoid making him feel jealous."

"Some people are jealous when they have no reason to be. Who can explain it?" She shifted in her chair and her shoulders slumped. "At least I don't have that problem. My man doesn't care what I do as long as I leave him alone."

"Does he come to church with you?"

One side of Marcy's lip curled up and she tittered. "Not that man. Horses couldn't drag him to church. I know. Since I became a Christian several years ago, I've tried my best to get him here. Heaven knows he needs the Lord."

"Oh. How sad that he won't listen and come with you."

She shrugged. "Yeah. I've quit trying. No use in wearing myself out pleading and begging. May as well let it go."

Lillian saw Thomas look around for her. "Guess I'd better go. I'll pray for you and your husband."

Marcy lifted a hand. "Thanks. I'll pray for you and yours."

All through the meal, Thomas showed attention to Lillian. He served her refills of iced tea, cut a dessert for her, and brought her seconds when she ran out of Mexican Corn Casserole. A few women looked at her with envy, but most seemed glad to welcome her back into their conversations. She helped clean the kitchen while Thomas visited with the menfolk, and he chatted as they drove home afterward. She had enjoyed their day together.

Later, while Thomas viewed his favorite detective show, Lillian wrote in her journal.

Father in Heaven: I'm grateful to You for the life You've given me. I'm thankful for my husband and my home. Thank you for my good health. I know I haven't had the best attitude, and sometimes, I'm not appreciative of what I have. Sometimes, my thoughts are negative. Sometimes I think badly about other people. I'm sorry, Jesus. I want to do better. I want to love like You love. I want to spend my life doing good for others, helping someone who has a hard life or who is going through a hard time. My life isn't worth much if I spend it selfishly. Please show me how I can help others. Amen

She knelt beside the bed and prayed for Marcy and her husband.

TWENTY-SIX

The following Wednesday at the *lieu de encontre*, Lillian told the girls what had happened the previous Wednesday.

"I didn't lie," she said, "but if he had pressured me like he usually does, I would have been in trouble. I don't know what he'll do if he ever finds out about our meetings."

"Oh, that was close," said Kora. "You mean he didn't pressure you? Isn't that unusual?"

"Yes, it is. But what happened at the dinner Saturday blew my mind." She told them about Thomas's Orange Chicken and Victoria.

"Wow!" said Kora. "Thomas is changing, isn't he? I saw what happened. Boy, Victoria was steamed!"

"I can see some change in him," Lillian said, "but not entirely. I'm realizing something, though. We girls need to change."

Bella leaned forward. "Change? How do you mean?"

"I realized last week that we have been gossiping and bad-mouthing our husbands and other people. That is as wrong as what our husbands are doing."

Kora sat up straight. "How can that be as bad as what they're doing to us? What they're doing is abuse."

133

"Yes," Lillian said. "I don't mean to be preachy, but remember what Pastor Bill said a while back — that to God, sin is sin. There are no little sins or big sins. The Bible lists gossipers along with those who hate God, deceitful people, and those who are evil. I looked it up. It's bad, ladies."

Bella and Kora looked at each other and then back at Lillian. "Of course, you're right," Kora said. "I've been going home feeling guilty when we talk ugly about people and our husbands."

"Me, too," Bella said. "I don't want to dishonor God by being a gossiper."

Lillian and Kora both nodded.

"I think we need to pray. I need to repent." Bella reached for their hands, and they prayed together. Wiping away tears, they hugged each other.

"We'll need to hold each other accountable," Kora said. "If you hear me gossiping or bashing my husband, please stop me."

"Me, too," said Lillian. "If I start dissing Thomas, remind me to stop."

"I agree," said Bella. "We'll have to stick together and help each other." They nodded their agreement.

"Have you been writing prayers in your journals?" Lillian pulled out her floral journal.

"I wrote something, but it isn't a prayer. More like wishful thinking." Kora opened her journal and read.

Dear Journal: Life is sometimes hard, but it's also wonderful. It's like a planet in the universe, spinning out of control but, at the same time, performing its job. But—what are planets created to do? Just orbit around in the cosmos for eons? What am I created to do? Clean the house, do the laundry, cook the meals, and then start all over again? Is that all my life will ever be?

I have dreams. I want to learn new things. I want to have a family. I want to see the world. At least more than I see sitting in this house day after day. I've heard and read so much about our beautiful world, and I need to experience more of it. I'd like to visit the Grand Canyon. The Petrified Forest. Go deep-sea fishing. See polar bears in Antarctica. Bears in Alaska. Elephants in Africa. **The** Matterhorn in Switzerland. I want to love and be loved by people around me. I want to get to know my neighbors. I want to volunteer at the local food bank or serve Thanksgiving dinner to those who need help. I want to honor God by doing something of value for other people. I want my life to mean something.

"Oh, Kora!" Lillian pressed her hands against her cheeks. "Your life does have meaning!"

Kora's big eyes seemed to search for an answer in Lillian's face. "Is there hope, Lillian? Will anything change? I feel like my life is passing while I'm doing nothing."

Lillian stood and began to pace while Bella moved closer to Kora and put her arm around her shoulders. Lillian stopped in front of the two younger women and stared at them.

"There is hope," she said. "We can't lose track of that. We must remember that God is working on our behalf. His Word tells us that he will honor us when we honor Him, so our primary purpose is to honor God." She snapped her fingers. "I almost forgot to tell you. I talked to Marcy at church, and she's unhappy with her marriage. I told her we'd pray for them."

"Who's Marcy?" Kora asked.

"She's the quiet lady that sits in the back. You seldom see her talking to anyone. I get the feeling she's in a desperate situation."

"I'll sure pray for her," Bella said. She leaned back and chewed on a fingernail. She opened her mouth to speak and then closed it.

"Okay, Bella, spit it out," said Lillian. "Something is on your mind."

"I have to tell y'all something." Bella turned her face away. "Remember when I said I'm afraid Levi will do something bad? Well, he has." A sob rose from her chest.

Kora and Lillian looked at each other. "What did he do?" Lilian asked.

Bella broke down and cried. "He had an affair."

Kora rushed to her side to comfort her. "Oh, no."

Lillian put a hand over her mouth. "Oh, oh, oh," she said. "I can't believe he did that. When did you find out?" She handed Bella a napkin to use as a tissue.

Bella mopped her face. "My sister-in-law called me yesterday and told me, so I confronted him last night, and he admitted it."

"What are you going to do?" Kora asked.

"I d—d—don't know. He said he'd give me a divorce if that's what I want." She inhaled deeply and exhaled. "I don't know what I want." She broke down again. "I want this never to have happened. How could he do this to me?"

Her friends comforted her the best they could while she sobbed.

Lillian spoke gently. "Do you know who she is? Is he going to stop seeing her?"

"I don't know her." Bella hiccupped. "He said he wouldn't see her again. I don't know if I believe him."

"Do the kids know?" Kora asked.

"No, and I can't tell them. I'll leave that up to him. Or until he leaves me if that's what he chooses."

Lillian and Kora comforted her until they each had to return home.

TWENTY-SEVEN

The few weeks, Bella cleaned, did laundry, and cooked meals as though she were in a stupor. When she passed the mirror in the hall, her reflection reminded her of a zombie she'd seen in the movies, with red-rimmed eyes and sunken cheeks. She couldn't eat and slept little. She did the housework without thinking, moving as though her body had been programmed to cook, clean, and do laundry. When the kids needed something, she responded, mostly without words. Levi looked at her out of the corner of his eyes but said nothing.

Then things worsened. She slept on the couch every night, making sure to rise before her family to make breakfast. His drinking increased until he fell into bed late, inebriated, and often still dressed. He growled at her and the kids until she threatened to kick him out of the house and change the locks.

At their meetings on Wednesdays, she cried, and the ladies cried and prayed with her. "Something has to change," she said. "I can't keep living like this. It's affecting the kids. Trevor doesn't even want to come home, and Addie stays in her room. I don't want my kids to have to live in a home with this kind of abuse."

One day, Levi came home early from work. When she asked him why, he snarled and slapped her. "Why don't you tend to your own business?" he said with a curse. "And by the way, you'll need to ask for more hours at the hospital. I won't be going back to work for a while." He took a swig of beer.

Bella brushed tears from her stinging, red face. "Why?"

He cursed again. "I done told you to tend to your own business."

Her eyes widened, and she whispered. "Please tell me you didn't get fired."

He snickered. "Okay, I won't tell you. I'll tell you this, though. You'd better ask for more hours at the office if you plan to pay the bills and feed your kids."

She lashed out. "Didn't your parents teach you to be a responsible adult?"

"Huh!" His nostrils flared. "My parents didn't teach me anything. I've always been a free spirit, free to come and go as I please, and I'm not gonna change now."

Bella finished cleaning the kitchen after supper and went to bed. Levi would be up late drinking and wouldn't go to bed until late, if at all, so she decided to sleep back in their bed. She wiped away tears as she picked up her journal.

~~Dear Journal~~ Father God: I don't know what to do. I will request more hours at work, but that won't be enough. We'll be without health insurance now. My work only covers me, not the family, and I can't afford to pay out of pocket. Our debts aren't many but paying them all and buying groceries will be a stretch. I won't be able to buy beer and cigarettes for Levi. That'll make him mad as all get out.

Will you please help me? I can't do this by myself. I have two kids—now three—to support. Of course, Lord, You already know all this. Would it be wrong for me to kick him out? Will he ever change? I understand you won't force him to change, but I wish you would. I miss the old, hardworking, sweet, and caring Levi. Will you please bring that Levi back to me?

She closed the journal and slept. Her dreams were filled with face of a young Levi that morphed into a monster that chased her until she finally woke, weary and depressed.

The next day, she requested more hours at work, and they hired her full-time. As a full-time employee, she would get more benefits, including a health insurance family plan, which made up for a little of her disappointment about the extra work. She expected no help from Levi even if he stayed home all the time. Most likely, he would drink himself into a stupor and then sleep the rest of the day. She made a deal with her boss to work every other Saturday so she could be off every other Wednesday. That would give her at least two Saturdays a month with her kids and two Wednesdays to meet with her friends. Since their meeting didn't last all day, she would have the rest of the day to clean and work around the house and be there with the kids.

When she returned home from work, Levi rummaged around in the refrigerator. "I'm hungry," he yelled. "Why don't you have supper ready?"

She pushed him out of the kitchen. "Because I just got home from work," she said. "I haven't had time to fix supper."

He fell back into his recliner and started flipping through the TV channels. She pulled out ground beef from the refrigerator and threw it on the counter with some pasta and tomato sauce. Listening to him sputtering something about women, she stabbed a butcher knife through a head of lettuce and issued her own tirade about men until something pricked at her heart.

"Listen to you," a little voice inside her spirit said. "You aren't responsible for him, but you are responsible for you." She thought she recognized Lillian's voice in her head.

She stirred the browning ground beef and checked the pasta pot. It boiled, just like her temper. Whack, whack, whack. Lettuce, cucumbers, and onions flew off the chopping block onto the countertop. She scraped them up and flung them into a large bowl. Once again, she stirred the ground beef and threw spaghetti into the boiling water. When she finished the meal, she called her family for supper.

"This smells so good, Mom," Addie said. "I love your spaghetti." She bowed her head for the blessing and then filled her plate.

"Me, too," Trevor said, piling his plate high with spaghetti, salad and garlic bread. "Mom is a good cook, right, Dad?"

Levi reached for the salad as he rolled bloodshot eyes toward Bella. "Oh, yeah, she certainly is," he said. "Don't you know that's why I married her?"

"Really?" Addie looked at Bella. "Is that true, Mom?'

"I don't know," Bella said. "I always thought he married me for my money. Or my looks. Maybe both."

Tyler laughed. "Mom, did you used to have lots of money? Or do you have some we don't know about?"

"I know she has beauty," Addie said. "Mom, you're beautiful."

Bella smiled at her kids. "Thanks, Addie. And no, Trevor, I've never had any money to speak of."

"Your mom is beautiful and a great cook, but she's a little short when it comes to finances. Of course, I've made most of the money in this family. A person can't make much by working only two days a week."

Bella rolled her eyes. "I worked only two days a week because you wanted me to stay home and keep house so you wouldn't have to. Not to mention taking care of those animals of yours."

"Yeah, I guess that's true," Levi said. "Keeping house is woman's work. You hear that, Trevor? Never forget it."

Bella glanced at her son, who frowned at his dad. "Trevor, you learn to respect women and remember that if they work to provide part of the income for the home, you are responsible for your part of the housework."

Levi slurped his spaghetti, slinging red sauce all over the table. "Don't you listen to her, son. Never be caught doing women's work." He wiped his face on his shirt sleeve. "Now that your mama is a full-time employee at that hospital, we'll see the dough rolling in." He poked her shoulder with a sauce-covered finger. "Won't we, sweetheart?"

She glanced at his sauce-spattered shirt. "Yeah, sure. Especially since you're no longer working, money sure will be rolling in."

"Why aren't you working, Dad?" Trevor asked. "Did you quit?"

Levi's face darkened, and he shoved his plate, spilling his food on the table. He grabbed his bottle of beer and stood, knocking his chair over. "Yeah, so what? Working at a dead-end job is not for me. No way. I'm gonna get a better job—one where I can get ahead. Maybe be a boss or something. You wait and see." He staggered back to his recliner and turned the TV up.

"I'm sorry, kids," Bella said. "I shouldn't have said anything."

Addie hugged her. "It's okay, Mom. It isn't your fault."

"Don't worry none, Mom," Trevor said. "He'll be all right. And we're fine, ain't we, Addie?"

Addie nodded, then turned to her brother. "Aren't we," she corrected.

"I said we're fine, and I meant it."

Bella smiled at the misunderstanding and started to clear the table. Addie and Trevor helped her clean the kitchen before they retired to their rooms.

TWENTY-EIGHT

"Oh, Bella! We missed you last week." Kora squeezed Bella in a big hug when they met in their *lieu de rencontre.*

"Me, too. Now you gotta tell me everything I missed." Bella wrinkled her nose. "I hate that I'll miss every other Wednesday, but at least I have that."

"We don't have much to tell you," Lillian said. "Nothing much happened."

Kora nodded. "Yeah. We have the same boring lives we had the week before. What about you? Sounds like you've gone through some unpleasant things."

Bella slumped on the log. "Girls, I don't know what I'm going to do. Levi got fired, so I'm having to work full-time now. Of course, you already know that."

"We got your message that you've started working full-time, but we didn't know why," said Lillian. "Do you know why he was fired?"

"Not really. He won't talk about it. I imagine because of his drinking. Now he stays drunk most of the time."

"That makes me so mad!" Kora hugged her friend. "Is there anything we can do? Of course, we're praying for you and Levi."

"Is he helping at all around the house since you're working full time?" Lillian pushed Bella's hair back from her face. "I can't help but worry about you."

"Of course not." Bella leaned back and rested her head on the log behind her. "I sometimes wish I were a redbird so I could hide in the leaves when things get rough."

Kora looked up. "You know, you might want to be a sparrow instead. I'd think a redbird would have a hard time hiding."

Bella laughed. "You would think of that, Kora. I guess as big as I am, I might have a hard time hiding. Maybe I should wish to be a fox or groundhog so that I could burrow in the ground."

Lillian heaved a big sigh. "You know, it doesn't matter what we are, seems like we all have things to deal with. Of course, some more than others. I just think it's such a shame that we have to deal with the selfishness of other people. Why should we have to suffer from their selfish choices? If Levi chooses to drink, Bella shouldn't have to suffer from it. Let him suffer the consequences of his own actions."

Bella and Kora turned to look at Lillian.

"That may be true, Lillian," Kora said, "but how can we make that happen? How can we avoid the consequences of our mates' behaviors?"

"Hmmm." Bella straightened her back. "Maybe I should stop doing for him. Let him cook his own meals, wash his own clothes, and pick up his own messes. Humpf!

His messes would never get picked up, so I'd suffer from that!"

"But," Kora said, "you could stop cooking for him. Maybe there are other things he depends on you to do for him."

"It's certainly a thought," Bella said.

"I can't stop cooking and cleaning at my house," Kora said. "Since I don't work outside the home, that's all I'm responsible for. I can't think of any way to change my situation."

"Other than calling the abuse hotline," Lillian said. "That might be a thought."

Kora nodded. "Believe me, I've thought of that a few times. But when I think about how my life would be affected, I don't know if I want to go that route. I just want him to love me the way I love him. I know I can make that happen. I'm losing weight and working on keeping my mouth shut when he gets angry. I'm trying not to provoke him."

"I always think of the kids," Bella said. "What will happen to them if I leave Levi? I want them to grow up seeing what a good marriage can look like."

"I'm glad my kids grew up seeing a good marriage," Lillian said. "Now they don't know what's going on. They only know I'm different, and they don't see much of me. I know they'd rescue me in a heartbeat, but I got myself into this and have to get myself out of it. I often think God is allowing me to handle it myself since I didn't ask for His wisdom before I married Thomas."

"Why didn't you?" asked Kora. "It doesn't seem like you not to do that."

Lillian heaved another sigh. "Stupidity. He claimed to be a Christian. He acted so charming and was such a prominent figure in our community. He met all the criteria of good husband material. At least that's what I thought. Boy, was I ever wrong."

Bella leaned back against the log. "Looks like we've all messed up and married the wrong men. Too bad."

"Yeah," Kora agreed. "Too bad for us. I hate to think my life will be this way forever. But even if I left Nathan, no one else would have me."

"What makes you think that?" asked Lillian.

"Nathan tells me that all the time. He says, 'You'd better not leave me 'cause nobody else would want you.' One minute, he calls me beautiful, and then he turns around and says I'm dumb and ugly."

Lillian gasped. "Kora! You're beautiful, intelligent, and gifted. You have a lot to offer." She stood. "Look, girls, I know what it is to have a good husband. Jim truly loved me and made me feel loved. These men are putting us down to control us. We can't allow them to make us feel less. When they belittle us, we must be strong and tell ourselves we are worthy of real love. I'm telling both of you now that you are worthy of love."

Kora jumped up. "I can see that. We should start writing positive statements about ourselves in our journals."

"That's a good idea," Bella said.

"Oh, and I have a suggestion," Kora said. "Lillian, what if we meet only every other Wednesday so Bella doesn't feel left out?"

"I think that's a good idea," Lillian said. "We can use the other Wednesday to pray for Bella while she's working."

TWENTY-NINE

"Where have you been?" demanded Levi when Bella arrived home in the middle of the afternoon. "I haven't had anything to eat, and I'm hungry."

"That's too bad," she answered. "Why didn't you fix yourself some lunch? You have nothing else to do."

"It's your job to cook for me," he shouted. "Now get in the kitchen and fix me some food."

"No, I'm not going to do that." Bella threw a bag of groceries she had purchased after the meeting onto the counter. "I have housework to do since I now have two full-time jobs. Looks like you didn't do anything. You're an able-bodied adult. Fix your own food. I have to wash your clothes, clean your messes, and care for your children. The least you can do is fix your own food." She whirled and headed for the laundry room. She shoved a load of towels into the washer along with detergent. Next, she started cleaning the bathroom. She could hear him muttering and rattling dishes in the kitchen.

"Dear Lord, give me wisdom and patience," she prayed as she worked. When she noticed the quiet in the kitchen, she peeped in. He sat at the table, eating some cold spaghetti and a bag of chips. She planned to make fried chicken for supper for herself and the kids. If he stuffed himself now, he likely would be asleep by the time they ate. That would be fine with her.

Sure enough, he had collapsed in his recliner and snored loudly by the time Bella and the kids fixed supper.

"Want me to wake Daddy?" asked Trevor .

"No, let him be," Bella said. "He ate earlier, so he won't be hungry." She walked into the living room and turned down the TV. She pulled the window shades. He could sleep there all night and let her sleep in peace in the bedroom. Her body needed the rest, and she needed some alone time.

They ate all the chicken, and Bella threw the leftover potatoes and bread to the animals. Soon the kitchen sparkled, and they retired to their rooms. The kids had homework, and Bella picked up her journal.

Dear Journal: I enjoyed my day off, even though it isn't really a day off when I have to spend it cleaning the house. Since I'm a homebody, though, I do love to be home.

Today, I realized something. Right now, I feel like crap. I feel unloved, unworthy, ugly, and stupid. But I'm starting to understand that none of this is true about me. God made me beautiful. I am intelligent. I am competent. I'm not bragging since I understand that God gave me everything I have and made me what I am.

From now on, I will believe that. No more putting myself down. No more thinking bad of myself. I am worthy of love, and I will love others even when they don't act loveable. Love is a choice, and I will choose to love.

She put down her journal and went to her sewing machine. She had started sewing a dress Addie needed for a school activity, and she had to get it done. She could rest later. Now that she worked full-time, she didn't have time to do everything that needed done. She squinched her eyes and rubbed them. Then she flipped the bodice wrong side out to finish it.

"Addie," she called. "Come try this on. I need to make sure it fits before I sew on the skirt."

Addie pulled on the bodice and looked into the mirror. "Mom! This isn't right. This looks like something for a little kid.

I'm not a little kid."

Bella groaned. "Addie, I thought you liked this pattern."

Addie pulled the top off and threw it down. "I don't like this material. I wanted green, not pink. And I don't like that collar. My friends will laugh at me if I wear this." She burst into tears.

"Oh, Addie. I'm so sorry." Bella put her arms around her daughter. "Don't worry, I can fix it. I think." Addie ran from the room, and Bella buried her head in her hands. Just another thing to worry about.

She picked up her journal and read her last entry. She straightened her shoulders and lifted her chin. She could do this. She would stop on the way home the next day and choose more fabric and a different pattern. Her daughter would have a dress she would wear proudly to her school function. She would see to it. Tonight, she would get some much-needed sleep. That would make her feel better tomorrow.

THIRTY

*L*illian had supper ready when Thomas arrived home from work. He explained that an employee issue caused him to be late. She could see his bad mood when he entered the back door. She ran to kiss him, but he shoved her away and threw his briefcase on the counter.

"It's Tuesday, so I made meatloaf."

"Why are you stuck in such a rut?" he roared. "Maybe some days I'd like something else to eat."

"But you always want meatloaf on Tuesdays. I like to fix what you want."

"Well, today I don't want meatloaf. I don't even like your meatloaf. Can't you see that I seldom eat it? A monkey could make better meatloaf than you." He stomped off into the living room, plopped into his recliner, and turned on the TV.

Stunned, Lillian stood in the middle of the kitchen. When they first married, he wrote out his menu for every week. Almost always the same. It had been like that for all their married life. Now, what was she to do?

She pulled the meatloaf from the oven, slapped a lid on the pan of mashed potatoes, and opened the refrigerator. She dragged out a container of sliced ham, a tomato, and a head of lettuce. She slapped together a ham sandwich, put it on a plate, and poured a glass of tea.

"Here is your supper," she called, placing it on the table with a napkin. On her way to the bedroom, she passed him as he entered the kitchen.

He gasped. "Where are you going?" he called.

"To the bedroom. Hope you enjoy your supper. I'm done."

"Oh, no, you're not done, woman. You come back in here and have supper with me."

She ignored him. Then she heard him stomp across the floor. Tensing, she refused to look at him when he entered the room. He grabbed her hair and twisted her head around.

"Look at me," he bellowed. "I'm your husband, and you're my wife. I speak, and you answer. GOT IT?" He started dragging her across the room. Finally, she managed to get to her feet, and he let go of her hair. He shoved her into the kitchen and toward the stove. "Since you made meatloaf, that's what we'll have." He grabbed two plates and forced them into her hands.

She filled the plates with the supper she prepared and set them on the table. He grabbed her arm and pulled her into a chair. "Now, eat!" he ordered.

She fought to maintain her composure. Tears tried to surface, but she squeezed her eyelids closed, denying them. She lifted her chin, straightened her back, and picked up her fork. She took a bite and forced a smile. "Ummm! It's good meatloaf," she said. "I think I did a pretty good job of making it. What a shame you can't enjoy it."

He blinked and looked down at his plate, then back at her. She continued to eat and smile at him between bites.

Finally, he picked up his fork and took a bite of meatloaf. "Hmmm." He nodded. "It is good." He took a few bites of potatoes and corn. She didn't flinch when he placed his hand over hers. "Darling, I'm sorry to be so rough on you. You know I get angry when you act rebellious. I can't stand for you to back-talk me."

She swallowed hard and pulled her hand from under his. "Like it makes me angry when I work to prepare the meal you requested only to have you belittle me for it?"

"Belittle you?" He jumped up. "Belittle you? You know my expectations. When I come home after working hard all day and putting up with a lot of crap from those idiots I work with, I expect to come home to a sweet wife who pleasures in making me happy. Can you understand that?" He shoved his plate off the table. Broken glass and food spattered across the floor. He walked through it, tracking glass, potatoes, corn, and meatloaf through the kitchen and into the living room.

She sat still for a while with her eyes squeezed closed. She whispered a prayer and then started cleaning up the mess. She shook her head when a song stirred in her head. It grew louder until she thought Thomas surely heard it. A quick glance into the living room—no, he drowsed in the recliner. She started humming the tune. Maybe the brokenness inside her, which had caused bitter tears to flow night after night, had started to mend. How could she feel a song after what she'd just experienced? She hummed louder as she moved to pick up shards of glass and kernels of corn. She wiped up tracks of potatoes and greasy meatloaf with a damp towel. She filled a bucket with warm water and mopped the floors.

"Great is thy faithfulness," she hummed. When she finished cleaning the mess, she raised her head and lifted her voice. "Morning by morning, new mercies I see: all I have needed thy hand hath provided--Great is thy faithfulness, Lord, unto me!"

She stood, amazed at the joy rising within. Could she have joy in her heart after what he did to her? Yes, she could. She recalled the Bible verse that says, 'The joy of the Lord is my strength.' She laughed as she poured dirty water down the sink. He could hurt her body, but with the strength that only came from God, she would not allow him to break her spirit.

She turned to see him standing in the doorway, looking at her. She forced a smile. He returned to his recliner and the TV, and she hummed a few more bars. "Pardon for sin and a peace that endureth," she sang. "Thine own dear presence to cheer and to guide, strength for today and bright hope for tomorrow, blessings all mine, with ten thousand beside." Oh, her God never failed! She never thought she could feel this way.

For the rest of the evening, he sneaked glances at her as she hummed the tune quietly from her chair across the room. At bedtime, he sat on the edge of the bed as she donned her thin, soft blue nightgown. When she lifted the covers to slide in beside him, she could feel his stiffness. Evidently, he didn't know how to respond to her new demeanor. She turned toward him and snuggled close. She lifted her head and kissed him on the cheek. He turned his back to her, and she lay still. Then suddenly, he turned toward her and embraced her. She forced herself to relax and accept his affection. He pulled her closer and kissed her hard until it hurt. She pulled back.

"You're hurting me," she said.

He let go. "I'm sorry. I didn't mean to hurt you."

Again, he pulled her close and kissed her, this time tenderly. Fighting her emotions as she remembered the ugly words and abusive actions of her husband, she responded to his lovemaking with silent forgiveness and a love she didn't feel. She prayed that someday, she would feel the love a wife should feel for her husband. In the meantime, she would choose to love.

THIRTY-ONE

"I think it's time we talk to Pastor Bill," Lillian told the girls at their next meeting. "Maybe he can get through to our husbands."

"Someone needs to get through to them," Bella said. "I'm not sure I can take much more. I'm so tired I can hardly function. I know I'm cranky with the kids, and I hate that. They deserve better. It's bad enough they have a dad who is mean to them the few times he pays attention to them at all. Now he's started hitting me, and I'm afraid he'll start hurting the kids."

"Oh, no." Lillian patted her hand. "I'm so sorry, Bella. That's it, then. We'll talk to Pastor."

Kora agreed. "That's a good idea. Maybe he can get them to see what they're doing to us. I'm sure Nathan would change if he understood how he makes me feel."

Lillian turned to Bella. "Could you drive us to the church office at our next meeting? Kora and I can walk to your house, and we can go from there. I'll call Pastor Bill to set it up."

Two weeks later, the three women met with Pastor Bill in his office at the church. He offered them coffee and waited for them to explain their visit.

"Pastor Bill," Lillian said, "we have problems and need your help. We don't know what to do."

"Yes, and it's bad, sir." Kora blushed. "We're desperate for answers."

Bella sat nodding.

Pastor Bill looked from one to the other. "Lillian, you want to tell me what's going on?"

Lillian twisted her wedding ring and wiggled in her chair. "Of course." She pulled a tissue from her pocket and wiped her eyes. "It's our husbands, Pastor. We all have serious problems with our husbands."

Pastor Bill frowned and adjusted his tie. "Uh, what do you mean? What problems do you have with your husbands?"

"They're mean to us." The words spilled from Kora's mouth. "Really mean. They abuse us. They won't let us do anything or go anywhere. We're like prisoners in our own homes."

Pastor Bill's eyes widened, and his jaw dropped. "What?" He jumped to his feet. "What are you talking about? You can't be serious."

"We are very serious," Lillian said. "What Kora's saying is true, Pastor."

Pastor Bill sat back down and forced a tight smile. He picked up a stack of papers and rearranged them. "Now, ladies, what you're saying can't possibly be true. You're just misunderstanding your husband's actions." He looked at Lillian. "Why, Thomas is a prominent man in our community and church. People around here look up to him. It's unthinkable to accuse him of such a thing. What would folks think?"

Lillian's eyes flashed, and her eyebrows raised. She stammered. "I—Pastor—I don't care...."

Bella put a hand on Lillian's arm and leaned forward. "Do you see this, Pastor?" She stood and lifted her arm, pointing. "How do you explain these bruises on my arm? Do you think I did that myself?"

Kora leaned forward and pulled up her sleeves to reveal

bruises on her upper arms.

Pastor leaned over to look at the bruises, then looked hard at Bella. "Bella, you want to be a witness to your husband, right? Get him into church. Get him to stop drinking and be a better husband, right?" She nodded. "Well, then," he said, "you must be patient with him and believe that God is working on him. He can't be all that mean. He isn't a bad guy. I've known his family for years. Be patient with him. Give him a little time."

He turned. "And, Kora, I've seen so much good in Nathan. I just can't believe that he's mean to you. He's an important part of our church. You should be supportive of him instead of accusing him of a few bruises. Maybe you got those from working in those pretty flower beds I've seen at your house."

All three women stared at him with open mouths. A deep blush crept up Pastor Bill's neck to cover his face. "Now, ladies, you can't lightly make such accusations toward your husbands. Think of what will happen if anyone hears what you're saying. If this ever got out, it would be impossible to stop the effect on our church and community." He rose and walked around his desk. "Oh, no, ladies. You three need to go home and be the good, submissive wives God called you to be. The Bible says you are to love your husbands and keep your homes. That means doing whatever is necessary to fix your marital problems. I've no doubt that if you will give your husbands the love and attention they need, everything will work out."

He was dismissing them! He would not listen. Would anyone listen to them and help them?

They were quiet on the way back to Bella's house. She invited them in for a quick lunch before they went home.

"So, now what are we to do?" Kora said. "I guess we're stuck for the rest of our lives."

"No, we're not." Lillian threw her bag on the counter and poured a glass of tea. "Pastor Bill is not God, and God is on our side. We're going to keep trusting Him. I know He will show us what to do and help us do it."

"I'm glad you have so much faith," said Bella. "I think my faith has all dried up."

"Yeah, me too." Kora balled up her fists. "I swear, if that man hits me one more time, I think I'll take a ball bat to his head."

"Wow, Kora," said Lillian. "You're getting violent. But maybe that's what we should do. Maybe we need to defend ourselves."

"And get beat half to death? Or killed?" A bitter snicker came from Kora. "There has to be a way we can get out with our lives and bodies still intact."

"Of course, we could divorce them." Bella looked sideways at Lillian. "That's an option."

"Is that what you want to do?" Lillian looked back and forth at the other two. "And you, Kora? Is that what you both want? It is an option. If that's what you want, I'll support you."

"How about you?" Kora asked. "Will you divorce Thomas?"

Lillian shook her head. "I've said before that I got myself into this and will suffer the consequences. If I had asked for God's wisdom before I married him, I'm sure I wouldn't have gotten into this mess. Now I'll trust God to show me the way out."

Kora picked up a napkin and wiped her eyes. "I wish I could figure out what Nathan wants. He tells me he loves me but then turns around and treats me like dirt. What do men want, anyway?"

"Huh!" Bella ripped her napkin in two. "I know what Levi wants. Beer. Sex. Food. A punching bag. That isn't hard to figure out."

"Jim told me once that men need to feel like the provider and protector of their families," Lillian said. "But in your case, Bella, Levi isn't being the provider or protector. Of course, his drinking gets in the way of that, right?"

"Yes. Before he started drinking so much, he did provide for us and protected us as well. He was a slob but a good husband and dad. I guess I didn't see that before."

Kora scowled. "You know, Nathan always tells me that it's his job to provide for me. Like that's important to him."

"Maybe we don't give them enough credit for doing that." Lillian bit her lip. "Maybe we need to praise them for doing such a good job. Without being patronizing, of course. We don't need to make it sound fake."

"I guess I'll have to skip this assignment," Bella said. "How can I praise my husband for doing a good job when he is being nothing but a leech on my kids and me? We do everything while he lies around drunk and nasty. When I leave for work every day, I don't want to go back. I go home only because of the kids."

Lillian and Kora hugged her.

"Why do you think he changed for the worst?" asked Lillian. "I mean, do you have any idea what the root of his addiction is?"

Bella looked at Lillian. "The root of his addiction?" She shook her head. "Isn't the root of everything sin?"

"Yes, but—I guess what I'm trying to figure out is—surely some certain decision caused him to get him where he is now. I don't know how to explain what I mean."

Bella covered her head with both hands. "I think I understand where you're trying to go. Thinking back, right after we married, he picked up a dirty magazine in a gas station and flipped through it. A little after that, he brought one home. Later, he started looking at porn on the internet. At first, I looked at it with him, but I found it repulsive, so I refused. That made him mad, and over the years, it escalated. A couple of years ago, he started drinking more and now he's had an affair. Since then, he's worse. Is that what you want to know?"

Lillian nodded. "So, the whole thing started with the porn. That addiction led to other problems."

"I guess. That seems like the way it started. I've always tried to get him to go to church with me, but he says the church is filled with hypocrites, and he's as good as anyone there, including me."

"Of course, a lot of people who stay away from church use that excuse." Lillian shrugged. "So sad. They don't understand that our salvation isn't based on how good we are."

"What are we going to do now?" Kora asked Lillian. "If Pastor Bill won't listen, who will?"

Lillian rose and paced the floor. She hugged herself and then ran her fingers through her hair. Bella and Kora were silent, waiting. A war raged within her — the same battle that raged inside each of them.

"I just can't believe he wouldn't listen," she said. "What's wrong with him? He defended our men without even listening to us or talking to them about the situation. Without even considering that we might be telling the truth." Then she stopped. "Have you girls been writing prayers in your journals?"

Bella and Kora looked at each other. "Some," said Kora. "But not much."

Balla blushed. "Once or twice," she said. "Since I've started working full time and still have to do all the housework and make supper, I'm worn out by bedtime. Then Levi's behavior stresses me out, so I don't even think about it."

"That's understandable," Lillian said. "I know this is hard on you, Bella. But if you could take a few minutes to write a prayer when you first get up and are fresh, I think you'd find it rewarding." She turned to Kora. "I think you and I can do extra on Bella's behalf for this assignment. Do you agree?"

Kora smiled at Bella. "You betcha, I agree. What you got in mind?"

"Let's do a fast. Let's fast for three days and believe God for a miracle for Bella. Actually, for all of us. Remember how Esther called a fast for the whole nation when the Jews were in danger of annihilation by Haman? We may not be that bad off, but I don't think God looks at the degree of trouble we're in. He loves us all and will help when we cry out to Him."

Kora's brows knitted. "Then I don't understand why He hasn't helped us. It sure doesn't seem like He hears me cry out to Him."

"I know," Lillian said. "I've felt that way, too. But I know He is faithful and true to His word. I won't turn from that truth. Maybe He's working on our husbands, but they won't listen. Maybe it will take Him longer than we hoped to get through to them."

"I guess." Kora pressed her hand to her lips. "I want to believe that He hears and answers me. Okay, Lillian, I'll do whatever it takes to get through to Nathan. So, what about this fast? How does it work?"

"For three days, we'll eat nothing, or at least very little. It won't be easy because our husbands may want us to eat with them, and they can't know what we're doing."

"I'll tell Nathan I'm on a special diet," Kora said. "Then he won't bug me about it."

"Now remember," Lillian said, "fasting doesn't mean just doing without food. It means praying a lot and praying hard. We have to pray specifically for our guys to listen to God when God speaks to them."

"I'll need prayers for myself, too," Kora said. "This will be a hard task. You can tell by looking at me that I like to eat."

Lillian and Bella laughed. "Yes, it won't be easy," Lillian said. "And remember, our men may get worse before they get better." Lillian tapped her fingers on the table. "But we'll get through it with God's help. Another thing is important. We must expect good things to come from our prayers."

"I'll pray hard, too," Bella said. "And I'll fast, too. My life depends on getting my husband to change."

"Great," said Lillian. "It may take some time, but this is going to happen. Faith will move mountains, and we will stand together in faith. God will move our mountains for us."

They joined hands and prayed together before they left for home.

THIRTY-TWO

*K*ora and Nathan went into town on Saturday to pick up some groceries. They were in the checkout line when a man pulled his cart in behind them. Nathan lifted a hand in a wave toward the man, and they discussed a recent televised ballgame. Nathan mentioned something about work as she busied herself with putting the groceries on the checkout counter. When they were driving home, Kora mentioned the man.

"Someone you work with?" she asked. "I thought you mentioned that his name is Mikie."

"Yeah. He's a good worker, but he's got some issues."

"Really?" Kora's eyebrows raised. "What kind of issues?"

"I think he's cheating on his wife. That poor woman. I've met her a time or two. She deserves much better."

"What makes you think that?"

"You know that woman that goes to your church—Victoria?"

"You mean our church."

"Yeah. Well, the other day, she came in to talk to him, and he acted embarrassed. He took her to his truck and talked to her. Then he kissed her. I've met his wife, and it wasn't her. Her name is Marcy."

"Wow. Does he know you saw him kiss her?"

"Yeah, I'm sure, and no, he didn't see me. I just happened to go to my truck to get a tool and noticed him. It's a shame, too. Marcy is a good woman. She supports him in all the crazy projects and hobbies he does that drain his bank account."

"That's awful! Then, they probably have financial problems."

"Oh, I'm sure they do. He's always trying to borrow money from everyone at work. He talks about losing his house or his vehicle if he doesn't get money to make the payments. There's always someone who will loan him enough to get him through the month."

"Does he pay them back?"

"Yeah, pretty much. People don't really like him, but they feel sorry for his wife. Some are getting tired of it, though, and refuse to help him out. He's always trying to sell something, like tools or equipment of some kind. The other day, he showed a picture of a table he wanted to sell. He even commented that Marcy would be mad if he sold it, but he didn't care."

"That's terrible. Poor Marcy."

"I'm pretty sure he's had multiple affairs. He considers himself a lady's man. When he's around women, he prances around and flirts like crazy. At the shop, he talks about women all the time. If they knew the way he degrades them, they'd have nothing to do with him. The rest of us get tired of it."

"I don't understand why anyone would cheat on a spouse. It doesn't make sense and is so hurtful."

"Yeah, it is." He looked at her. "Sweetheart, I will never cheat on you. I love you too much. You know that, don't you?"

She patted his leg. "Yes, I do, and you'd better not even look at another woman. That might be grounds for murder."

He laughed. "Yeah, I know you'd kill me if I did that. No worries, though, my dear. I'll stay faithful to you no matter what."

Recalling the earlier conversation with her friends, she forced a playful mood. "You'd better behave. I have contacts."

She winced when she saw his expression change. "What do you mean, you have contacts?" he said.

She slapped him on the leg. "Oh, you know I'm kidding. You don't even let me go anywhere. How could I have contacts? Duh."

"You griping about that again? How many times do I have to tell you it's for your own good?"

She looked out the passenger-side window and muttered. "Can't see how that benefits me."

"What'd you say?"

She turned back to him. "Did you see that big buck over there?"

He leaned over to look. "Oh, he's gone already," she said.

"I need a big buck in our freezer. I haven't been deer hunting in a long time."

"I don't care much for venison," she said. "By the way, have I told you how much I appreciate the work you do to provide for us? You are a good provider even if we don't have a buck in our freezer."

She could see his chest swelling, and a broad smile covered his face. "I try my hardest to provide a good life for you," he said. "I'm glad you finally appreciate it."

"I've always appreciated you. I just don't say it enough." She patted his leg again. "You're a good husband."

As they pulled into the driveway, he drew her close and kissed her before he opened the door. She finally understood what Lillian meant. He needed her to verbally appreciate his role as a husband. It was worth a try, even if it seemed a little egotistic to her. It wouldn't hurt her to stroke his ego once in a while. Come to think of it, she liked to have her ego stroked at times.

Together, they carried the groceries into the house and put them away. She would prepare a good supper for him tonight.

THIRTY-THREE

At church on Sunday, Bella pulled Lillian and Kora aside when she had a chance. "I'd like to visit Washington, D.C. in November."

"That would be nice," Lillian answered.

"Sure. Sounds fun," Kora said.

"I'm sorry," Bella said when they met at Kora's house Wednesday at eleven. "I had an errand in town and needed to get back home, so I thought it would be easier to meet here at eleven.

Lillian and Kora agreed to the plan. They each reported on their experiences from the last two weeks. Kora bubbled about her conversation with Nathan and how he received her compliment. Lillian had also brought a smile to Thomas's face with her praise. Bella remained quiet.

"Are you all right, Bella?" asked Kora. "Have you had a bad week?"

Bella shrugged. "Yeah. Pretty rough. I fasted and prayed all week, but if it's possible, Levi is worse. I don't know how much longer I can stand his abuse." She showed them bruises on her arms and neck and her blackened eye.

"Oh, Bella." Lillian pushed back a strand of hair from her face. "I didn't even see this." She gingerly touched the black eye with one finger. "Does it hurt much?"

"No. I tried to cover it with makeup," Bella said. "He's been so mean all week. I sent the kids to their grandma's because he's getting so rough. Trevor threatened to do something to hurt his dad." She shuddered. "I'm afraid he'll try something and end up hurt." She looked at Lillian. "Are you sure this fasting and praying will work?"

Lillian handed Kora the lunch basket. "I believe it will. Of course, we've discussed before that these guys have a will of their own, and God won't override them. Remember when I said things may get worse before they get better? Looks like they already have for you. Bella, I'm so sorry you're going through such a hard time."

Bella sniffed. "I think I'm going to leave him."

Lillian nodded. "You may have to for your own safety and for the kids. You can't afford to stay if he hurts you and them."

"You mean you approve of me leaving him?"

"Girl, it isn't up to me to approve or disapprove. You have to do what's best for you, and I will support whatever that is. I want you and your kids to be safe."

"But I don't want to make God angry."

Lillian gasped. "Oh, my goodness, no! You won't make God angry. Levi has been unfaithful to you, so you have reason to divorce him. And he is unfaithful as a provider and a protector. God says husbands are to love their wives as Christ loves the church. God loves you, and it isn't His will for you to be abused. Did he not take the marriage vows that he would love and cherish you, forsaking all others?"

"Yes, he did. In fact, our vows included honor and being faithful until death. But he has not kept those vows."

"Then he is not being a husband to you. Would you forgive him if he truly repented and changed?"

"Of course, I would. I made those same vows. I didn't vow to love him until he wronged me. I vowed to love him until I die. And I will. But I can't stay with him when he is hurting me and the kids."

Lillian nodded. "I don't think God wants you to. Again, I will support you in whatever decision you make."

Bella wiped her eyes and hugged Lillian. "I appreciate you so much. You always encourage me."

"Me, too," Kora said as she joined the hug.

Lillian laughed. "Okay, enough of that," she said. "I have a journal entry to read." She pulled out her book, opened it, and read.

Dear Journal: Life is too short to be lazy and live carelessly. Yet, I feel like I'm the worst kind of lazy. How do I help anyone? I can't minister to those I never talk to or see. What can I possibly do to change this? Yes, I can—and do—pray for people. I pray for my husband that he will be a light in someone's darkness and an example of your love to others. I pray for Pastor Bill and Katie as they help others and minister to people. I pray for those on the prayer list at church. But isn't there more I can do? I feel useless. God, please show me how I can do more for You.

"You help Bella and me," Kora protested.

"Actually, we help each other. But if Thomas reads this, he can't know about us, remember?"

"Oh, yeah," Kora said. "I'm the one who is useless. I don't help anyone. But God knows my heart. He knows I'd like to help others, and one day I will." She pulled out her journal. "I have an entry to read, too. It's a prayer." She opened it and read.

Dear Heavenly Father, I appreciate all you do for me. I especially thank You for my sweet husband, Nathan. He loves me so much. I know I don't do enough for him. And I know I don't do enough for You. I want to do more.

There's a lady at church—I don't know her name, but You know who I mean—the one who is always sad. I always smile at her. I don't know how to help her, so will You please? She must be alone since no one is ever with her. I hope she has a family that is good to her. If she doesn't, could you send her a good friend? No one should have to be alone.

There's also a little boy I'm concerned about. He always looks sad. I've noticed his parents hardly pay attention to him, and when they do, they're cranky with him. I hope they aren't mean to him. If they are, will You send someone to rescue him? I think he needs rescued. Amen

"How sweet," Bella said. "I know the little boy you're talking about. He has a lot of freckles, doesn't he? His parents treat him like they don't even love him. I wonder why."

"Yes, he's a cute, freckled face. I hope he isn't being abused," said Lillian. "Maybe we need to all pray for him and his parents."

"I sure will," said Bella. "I hate to see a child being mistreated."

"I think I know the woman you're talking about," Lillian said. "She's quiet and always sits near the back, right?" Kora nodded and Lillian continued. "Her name is Marcy. I talked to her one day at a church dinner. She is unhappy. She says she's tried to get her husband to go to church, but he refuses. I've been praying for her."

"I think she's a beaten-down woman," Kora said. "She has that look, if you know what I mean."

Lillian nodded. Then her eyes bugged. "I do know what you mean. You think we all have that look? I hadn't thought of that before."

Kora and Bella looked at each other and then at Lillian. "I hadn't either," Kora said. "You think other people see it when they look at us?"

"No," Lillian said, "not necessarily. I think you have to be a beaten-down woman to recognize another one. I think Marcy recognized it in me. She asked if Thomas is jealous. Seems like she saw something other people don't see."

"Wow." Bella shuddered. "That's kinda scary. I don't want

my face to show what I feel inside."

"I guess we need to make sure we smile a lot when we're in public." Lillian held out her hands to the other two. "And we'll pray for the peace of God to show on our faces instead of the turmoil we feel from our men."

THIRTY-FOUR

*D*uring supper that night, Lillian asked Thomas if he had noticed the little boy whose parents were inattentive and cranky with him.

"What caused you to notice that?" he asked. "I don't pay attention to people at church."

"Oh, I do. Especially children. I guess I'm a people watcher." She passed him the hot rolls. "Did you enjoy the baptism Sunday?"

"Oh, sure," he said. "I like stuff like that. Those people looked happy when Pastor Bill finished baptizing them."

"They sure did. Especially that young man. Were you baptized when you were a kid?"

His face reddened. "No."

"Oh. So, how old were you?"

The red on his face deepened. "Look. I joined the church to help me get elected to County Judge. It's important for my job. That's all."

"Really? You aren't a Christian?"

"Of course, I'm a Christian. My parents always took me to church, and now I go all the time. You know that."

"But just going to church doesn't make one a Christian. You have to accept Jesus and be born again. Haven't you done that?"

"You're asking personal questions, Lillian. I don't like to talk about my religion."

"Oh. I'm sorry. I didn't mean to embarrass you."

He threw his napkin down. "You didn't embarrass me. I'd just rather not talk about it. Can we change the subject?"

Lillian rose and picked up their plates. "Sure. Would you like some dessert? I made a creamy coconut cake today."

"Yes, I'd like that. Thank you." He took a large bite of cake and closed his eyes. "This is delicious. You make delicious desserts. In fact, you're a good cook." She refilled his coffee cup. "By the way," he said, "what's this about going to Washington DC in November?"

Lillian's head jerked around. "Oh, at our last dinner, Bella said she'd always wanted to go to Washington D.C. Maybe she is planning a trip there in November."

"I guess it would make a nice trip," he said. "Maybe we can go there sometime. In fact, I think I may have to go there for a conference before too long. Would you like that?"

"I would. That sounds fun. I'd also like to visit the Grand Canyon someday."

"Why? It's nothing but a hole in the ground."

"But according to the photos, it's a beautiful hole. It's a part of God's creation. I've read that the Petrified Forest isn't far from it. And the Painted Desert. I'd love to see those."

"Well, there's a lot of God's beautiful creation, but that doesn't mean we'll get to see it all. If I listened to you, we would spend every cent I make traveling around to see things."

"Oh, that would be so much fun. Maybe one day you'll retire, and we can travel."

He stared at her. "Are you serious? You think I'm old enough to retire?"

"One day you will be. Hopefully, we'll still be in good health and can go places."

"Maybe. I should have a pretty good retirement. Of course,

you'll have none."

"I worked long enough to have a little from the department store. If you'd allowed me to work longer, I'd have a nice retirement."

"Doesn't matter. You're not working as long as you're my wife." He stalked into the living room and switched on the TV.

Lillian picked up the romance novel she'd started and was soon immersed in the lives of Keatyn Griffin and Gareth Davenport. She finished the book, closed it, and then wrote in her Journal.

Dear Journal: Just finished a good book, *Keatyn's Journey*. I'm sure glad that girl finally got her thinking straight. Leah Brewer did a good job writing it. I may try to find more of her work.

On another note, I'm realizing we should be careful of our words. God created the world with words. He said, "Let there be..." and it happened. I'm starting to understand that we create our world with words. If I speak negatively, then my world will be negative. On the other hand, if I speak positive words, my world will be more positive. Yesterday, I said, "That tickled me to death." Then I remembered that the Bible says laughter is like medicine. I should never equate it with death because that's against what God says about it in the scriptures. So, I'll try to use another phrase to describe how I feel when I laugh. I want to learn more scriptures so I will never speak against what the Bible says. That's my sermon for the day. Ha ha!

She then picked up her Bible and concordance to search for information about marriage and divorce. Concerned about Bella, she sure didn't want to tell her wrong about divorcing her husband.

She searched scriptures about adultery. God gave infidelity as a reason for divorce, but why not abuse? Surely, He wouldn't want a woman to stay with an abusive husband.

She found verses telling husbands to love their wives as they loved themselves and to honor their wives. She found verses that said Christians are to get rid of wrath and anger and be kind to one another. She found a verse that said anger does not produce the righteousness of God. But what about a woman married to a man who isn't a Christian and is abusive? One verse says to pray to be delivered from wicked and evil people. She flailed out her hands. Isn't that what they were doing? She closed her Bible. Looks like they had to focus and pray hard to get these men saved.

She prayed. "Dear Lord, please help Bella know what to do. Please protect her and her kids from her husband. And dear Lord, show us how to get these men saved. They need You. Your Word says that You want people to turn from their evil ways and live. That's what we want, Lord. We're trying our hardest to repay evil with blessings because we believe that's what You want us to do. If they won't listen to You, please deliver us from their wickedness. I know You want to save them, and You're working on them. Show us what to do to help."

She drifted into a deep slumber until Thomas shook her. "Come on, sleepy head. Let's go to bed.

THIRTY-FIVE

*A*t the next meeting, Lillian arrived to find Kora and Bella with swollen eyes and red faces. She ran to them. "What in the world is wrong?" she asked.

Bella threw up her hands. "I'm done," she said. "I'm kicking Levi out and changing the door locks."

"What happened?"

"Levi hit Trevor. I won't stand for that. I called the kids' grandma to come get them and told him to get his stuff and leave. He'd better be gone when I get home."

Lillian turned to Kora, who wiped her eyes with a tissue. "I told Nathan I'm leaving," Kora said, "and he said he will kill me if I do. I'm scared."

Lillian gasped. "Wait—I thought Nathan was doing better. What happened?"

Kora sniffed. "He was. Things were so good. But all of a sudden, he reverted back to his meanness. He's meaner than he was before." She sobbed into her shirttail. "He said I would spend the rest of my life alone because no one would want me. He said he would make sure of that."

Bella gasped. "He said that? Good grief! That's mean. What are you gonna do?"

"I don't know. I dread even going back into that house. I dread him coming home from work. I'm tired of his narcissism and abuse. I'm sorry, Lillian. I've tried so hard. I don't know what to do. I've been asking God for His permission to leave, and I am determined to stay until I get it or he changes. It God gave me permission, wouldn't He make a way so I can? I don't want to be wrong in what I feel. I might want to leave so bad I'd just think God told me to. I don't want to do that."

Lillian hugged both of her friends. "Girls, I don't know what to say. I'm so sorry. I wish I could do something to help."

"You've helped us a lot," Bella said. "Now it's up to God to help us. I'm praying so hard for our husbands to get saved. Well, mine, anyway. I guess your husbands are Christians already."

Kora and Lillian looked at each other. "Actually," Lillian said, "I just found out that Thomas isn't. He thinks going to church makes him a Christian."

"Nathan does, too," said Kora. "Since he started going to church with me, he professes to be a Christian but has never made a confession of faith. And he hasn't been baptized. So how can he be? He isn't bearing the fruits of a Christian, either. I don't think a real Christian man would beat his wife."

"Being a Christian doesn't make a person perfect," Lillian said, "but I agree. Our men aren't bearing the fruits of a Christian. We've been praying for them, but evidently, they aren't listening to God. I don't know what else to do besides trust. And I know God is trustworthy."

Kora groaned. "It's so frustrating."

"Let me read you an entry I made in my journal," Lillian said. She read the one about speaking positive words.

"I've never thought about that," Kora said. "I'm bad about saying negative things. I'll work harder to correct that."

"Me, too," said Bella. "I guess even in a negative situation, I can speak positive words. Maybe it would help turn my negative situation into a positive one."

"That reminds me—I don't know how, but it does." Kora laughed. "I've learned some information about that letter we found. Nathan told me about this guy named Mikie at his work who is having an affair with Victoria from church."

"Really!" Bella said. "How interesting."

"Does Nathan know who his wife is?" asked Lillian.

"He said her name is Marcy. Said she's a good woman and faithful to him. Nathan said he's awful. A big flirt. Even the guys he works with don't like the way he acts."

"Marcy?" Lillian gasped. "She's the one we were talking about the other day. The woman at church. Remember?" She blew out a long breath. "I don't understand why men do that. Why can't they behave themselves and love their wives?"

"I don't understand either," said Kora. "Women don't do that."

"Well, some do." Bella twirled a strand of hair around her finger. "I heard about this guy who married a woman because she threatened to beat him up if he didn't."

Kora laughed. "Sounds like an interesting marriage."

"I think women do things differently," Lillian said. "They bully, but in a different way. I've seen them make men miserable if they didn't get what they wanted. Jim and I were friends with a couple who always seemed unhappy, and after we were around them a while, we noticed how she complained and nagged at him constantly. Even in front of us. No matter what he did, he couldn't please her. Jim took him out for lunch one day and talked to him. He said the man was jovial when his wife wasn't around. Jim called him a beaten down man. The man didn't say much about his wife, but he did insinuate that she made him feel less than a man."

"I guess it can work both ways," Kora said. "Guess I never thought about that behavior being equal to the bullying men do. I never thought about verbal and emotional abuse being as bad as physical abuse."

"But it is," Lillian said. "Our men not only physically abuse us—they also verbally and emotionally abuse us. When a person makes you feel like a nobody, that's abuse. And the way they belittle us with their words and actions, that's bullying."

"True," Bella said. "Levi makes me feel like I'm not worthy of his love and attention, so how can I be worthy of anyone's love? Even God's?"

Kora ran her fingers through her hair. "That's it. Exactly how I feel most of the time. And I'm tired of it."

Lillian inhaled and blew out her breath. "We gotta hang in there, ladies. We know we are worthy even when we don't feel it. We must know that."

THIRTY-SIX

A few days later, Thomas arrived home in a foul mood and started to take it out on Lillian.

"Who has been here today?" He came in like a storm. "Looks like tracks in the drive. You got a lover coming to see you?" He grabbed her arm and twisted it. Lillian jerked loose from his grasp, pulled herself as tall as she could, and narrowed her eyes.

"Only the man who came to pick up the goat you sold him. You're the one who made the deal with him, so you had to know about him coming."

"Are you sure he's the only one?" He looked her up and down. "Of course, I don't know anyone who'd want you."

"You can put me down, hit me, or even kill me, Thomas, but I'm not going to stand here and let you treat me like I'm a brainless nobody. When I said "I do" at the marriage altar, I didn't vow to become a punching bag. I promised to love and honor you for the rest of our lives, and so far, I have kept that vow. You made the same vow to me, but you have not kept it. You say you love me, but love doesn't give black eyes, bruises, and vile words. If you can't love and honor me, then there's nothing left to do but leave."

A wide-eyed Thomas stared at her like she was insane. She

entered the bedroom and came out a few minutes later carrying a suitcase.

"Oh, so you think you're really gonna leave me." He stood in front of the door.

"Yes, I am. I've had enough of your bullying." She set the suitcase in the middle of the room. "I'll walk into town and go see Pastor Bill. Maybe he'll believe me this time. Then I'll go see my kids until I can find a place to live. I can take care of myself."

"What do you mean, this time? Have you been telling lies to Pastor Bill?"

"No, not lies. It doesn't matter anyway, because he believes you are the cream of the crop in his congregation and in this community. Wonder what he'll do when he learns the truth?"

His jaw tightened, and his fists clenched. "Woman, how dare you speak bad about me to anyone, especially Pastor. I'll teach you...." He raised his hand over his head, and she instinctively ducked, then straightened to face him.

"Go ahead," she said. "I'm sure when he has to visit me in the hospital, he'll see you in a different light, especially when I call the police to report spousal abuse."

She turned toward the door. It might be a stretch, but if she could make him believe her, he would surely see that she was serious and see the need to change. If she did have to walk into town, she would go to Kora's until she could contact her kids. She had no doubt they would help her.

He grabbed her arm. "You're not going anywhere," he said through clenched teeth. "You'll stay here and apologize for what you've done. Then face the consequences."

"Oh, but I'll not stay here to be beaten again. I will leave. If not now, I'll wait until you're gone, then I'll leave. But I will leave. And once I'm gone, I won't be back."

His face contorted. "So, you're willing to make God angry? You know the Bible says God hates divorce."

"I didn't say I would divorce you."

"What's the difference? A wife is not supposed to be separated from her husband. I thought you were a good Christian woman."

"And I thought you were a good Christian man. The people in this community think you are, but they don't live with your abuse. If they did, they'd change their minds quickly."

"Humpf. You think people will believe you over me? I don't think so. I'm an important political figure around here."

Lillian shrugged. "It doesn't matter. I know, you know, and God knows. That's what matters." She picked up her suitcase and moved around him to walk out. He stretched his arm across the door, blocking her way.

She backed up and looked him in the eye. "Thomas, you may as well let me go. You have betrayed my trust, and I will leave. You can't keep me a prisoner here."

He moved his arm and, with a sweeping gesture, allowed her to go out the door. She breathed a sigh of relief when he didn't hit her. Without looking back, she walked down the steps and started down the road.

She reached the highway before she heard a vehicle behind her. She moved further into the leaves at the edge of the woods and continued to walk without looking around. A red car slowed, and the driver craned his neck to look at her. Lillian smiled and waved. He stopped the car and rolled down the window. "Need a lift?" he asked. She turned to look at a neighbor she had talked to a few times. "Everything all right? I can run you into town if you need."

"Yes, and no thanks to the ride." She smiled and waved him on. She waited until a couple of vehicles passed before she moved to walk on the grass beside the highway. The neighbors would be curious about her walking and carrying a suitcase. No doubt they would be spreading gossip all over the neighborhood.

In a few minutes, another vehicle approached. Without

turning, she recognized the sound of Thomas' truck. The vehicle ground to a stop, but she kept walking.

"Lillian, wait." She turned when she heard the door open. He stepped out and walked toward her. She drew back.

"I'm not going to hurt you," he said. "Will you please come back home? I need you and want you. Please, Lillian."

"Thomas, I told you I'm done. No more bullying from someone who professes to love me. You like to quote the Bible to me, but you don't live by what it says. Husbands are to...."

He interrupted. "Yeah, yeah, I know. Husbands are to love their wives as they love themselves. Husbands are to honor their wives as the weaker vessel. I know the words — I just don't do them. Trouble is, you're stronger than I am, and you're better. I've been a jerk, and I'm sorry. What can I do to make it up?"

"We've done the apology thing before," she said, "and it doesn't work. It has to be more than an apology. It has to be a sincere and real change. I can't continue to live like this."

"Like what?"

"Being afraid all the time. Dreading when your truck pulls into the driveway, and you come into the house. Not knowing what kind of mood you'll be in. Afraid to say anything that might make you angry, and never knowing what that is. Wondering if you've had a good day and we'll have a nice evening or a bad day, and you'll take it out on me. Just afraid all the time."

He gaped at her. "Is that what you've been? Scared of me? Dreading when I come home?"

She nodded and kept quiet. He bowed his head. "I'm so sorry, Lillian. I am so very sorry. If you'll come home, I'll be better. No more bullying. No more putdowns. I want you to know I do love you."

"Funny, I seldom feel love from you. Those few times you do show love, it feels nice, but the contempt I feel from you wipes those times away."

She raised her eyes to look into his. "Are you willing to change?" she asked. He nodded. "I'm talking about a real change. Not just words."

"What do you want me to do?"

She put the suitcase down. "I want you to go with me to see Pastor Bill. I want you to confess to him what you've been doing to me. I want you to confess to God and ask Him for help. If you do that, I'll stay, and we'll see what happens. Otherwise, I'm gone. I believe in second chances, but there is a line I won't let you cross, and we're about there."

He nodded. "Okay, I'll go see the Pastor." He took her arm. She started to jerk away, but he pulled away and then gently touched her again. This time, she yielded. "Lillian, I'm so sorry. I mean, I'm really sorry." He swallowed hard. "I don't know why I'm mean to you. You've been so good and loving to me. I don't want to be mean to you. Will you forgive me?"

"Yes, of course I will. But we will still see Pastor Bill. I'll call and make an appointment."

THIRTY-SEVEN

*L*ater that day, they sat in Pastor Bill's office. Pastor Bill looked from one to the other. "It's good to see you, Thomas. And you, too, Lillian." He shook their hands. "Thomas, I want you to know I'm so proud of you. You're doing a great job with the Service Outlook Committee." He looked at Lillian. "We've grown in that area, thanks to your Thomas. We are now involved in the local food bank and also the clothes closet, which helps a lot of people. A rehab program is moving in, and Thomas, you may want to look into that to see if we need to be involved."

Thomas nodded. "Sure, I'll get the information from you and check it out." He glanced at Lillian, who sat with her hands clasped in her lap.

Pastor Bill smiled and nodded. "But I know you didn't come here for that. How can I help you today?"

Thomas fidgeted, and Lillian looked at him, then down at her hands. He put one foot across his knee, then put it down. Pastor Bill waited for one of them to speak. Thomas leaned forward, resting his elbows on his knees, hands over his face. He raised his eyes to look at Pastor.

"Pastor Bill, I have something to tell you, but it isn't easy," he said. Lillian patted his hand. "I—I—uh—I haven't been honest with you. There's something I need to confess."

Pastor Bill leaned forward with his elbows on his desk. "Okay, Thomas. I'm listening."

"Well, the truth is, I haven't been a good husband to Lillian." He slipped his hands over his face again and drew in a deep breath.

"What do you mean?" Pastor Bill said. His eyes moved from one face to the other.

Thomas raised his head. "Pastor, I've been a bully to my wife. I've been mean and hateful to her. She doesn't deserve the treatment I've dished out. She's been a good wife to me, and I've sinned against her."

Pastor Bill's jaw dropped, and he jumped to his feet, staring at them. Lillian looked him in the eye but remained silent.

"Thomas, I hate to hear this. I—I don't know what to say."

Thomas took Lillian's hand. "She has put up with my abuse since we married. She's been supportive of me all the while I mistreated her." He rubbed his face again. "I'm so sorry for my behavior. I've apologized to her, and now I apologize to you. Pastor, I'm sorry. I want to change. What do I need to do?"

Pastor Bill drew in a deep breath. "This takes me by surprise, Thomas." He sat back in his chair. "Lillian, is this true? Has Thomas treated you badly?"

Lillian nodded. "Not only has he sinned against me but against God." She turned to Thomas. "Sweetheart, you've repented to me, and now it's time to repent to God."

"Yes, I know." Thomas wiped the tear that made its way down the side of his face. "I want God to forgive me."

"Then you need to tell Him," Pastor Bill said.

Thomas slid out of the chair to his knees, and Lillian and Pastor Bill knelt on either side of him. Pastor Bill led him through a prayer of confession and repentance. When he finally rose, tears streamed down his face, and his eyes shone. He grabbed Lillian and hugged her hard, then turned to hug Pastor

Bill. Lillian handed him a tissue, and after he mopped his face, he laughed.

"Wow. I feel different." He laughed and hugged Lillian again. Then they all laughed together. Chill bumps rose on her arms, and her heart rate increased as she realized what had happened. She grabbed a tissue from a box on Pastor Bill's desk and wiped her eyes. Still a little apprehensive, she stepped back as Thomas pumped Pastor's hand. Could a person really change instantly? She remembered changing after her conversion as a young teenager but couldn't remember how quickly the change happened. His face looked different. He almost glowed.

"Want to be baptized this Sunday?" Pastor Bill asked.

"I sure do," Thomas said. "And I want to start attending that New Converts' class you've mentioned. Will that be okay?"

"More than okay. That will be great." Pastor Bill handed him some literature for new converts and asked them to be seated.

"Now, Thomas," Pastor Bill said, "you are changed on the inside because Jesus moved in, but you will still have temptations. Your spirit has come alive, but your soul — your mind, your will, and your emotions — may sometimes want you to go back to your old ways. Remember, you are in control of them and will have to say no when your brain and your emotions try to persuade you to make wrong decisions. Do you understand?"

Thomas looked confused. "I'm not sure I do, Pastor."

Pastor Bill smiled. "People tend to think that when they give their hearts to Jesus, they become perfect. That isn't true. You still have the same emotions you've always had, but now you have the Holy Spirit to guide you to make the right decisions. But He won't force you. Your will is your own. When you feel angry at Lillian or something puts you in a bad mood, you may be tempted to fall back into the old ways of bullying and controlling, but now the Holy Spirit will prompt you to stop. Always listen to the little voice of your conscience and refuse to yield to that temptation."

Thomas slowly nodded. "That makes sense. I think I can do that."

Lillian shuddered. What if he did revert back to his old ways? No, she must have faith and patience. The change would come. She had to trust that.

"If you mess up once in a while, repent and try harder. Lillian and I will be praying for you. I think you'll see your wife differently now and won't want to hurt her. You're not the same man you were. I advise you to start studying the Bible and praying together every day. That will help strengthen you so you can resist any temptations."

Thomas looked at Lillian. "Think we can do that?" She nodded, and he looked back at Pastor. "Thanks for everything, Pastor. I never again want to treat my wife the way I've been treating her."

Pastor Bill looked at each of them. "Thomas, Lillian, would you both be willing to go to marriage counseling for a while? I know of a Christian counseling team who could help you. I think it would benefit you both and help you with some issues you may still need to deal with."

Thomas nodded. "Yes, I would appreciate that." He turned to Lillian, who was nodding, then back at Pastor. "Do we need to make an appointment?"

"No, I'll set it up and let you know." He smiled at them. "I think you'll be amazed at how much your lives will be changed after today, and especially with the help of this counselor. He and his wife are a team, and they will help you a lot. And I'm here if you ever need me, either one of you." He leaned slightly toward Lillian. "I'll be here for you, Lillian, I promise. I have no intentions of making the same mistake I made before."

She smiled as she took Thomas's arm and allowed him to

lead her to the vehicle.

All the way home, Thomas periodically laughed and shook his head. "Wow!" he kept saying. Lillian was sure he had changed inside, and she would no longer have to fear him. She had to believe that, because that's what she had prayed for since they first married.

THIRTY-EIGHT

When they attended church the following Sunday, Thomas stood next to Lillian as they chatted with the other parishioners, then sat with his arm around her the whole service. At the end of the sermon, Pastor Bill announced that they would be baptizing a new convert. When Thomas rose and went to the front, several people gasped, and one person commented, "I thought he was already a Christian." Lillian glanced back at Kora and Nathan. Nathan's eyes were wide and his mouth open, and a smile covered Kora's face.

Pastor Bill spoke to the congregation. "I'm like some of you — I had the misconception that Thomas here had been saved for a long time. Imagine my surprise when he came to my office to confess his sins. Imagine how happy the angels in heaven were to see a new soul saved. We need to join them in praising God for a lost soul that has been found."

The people applauded, and Thomas beamed. "There may be others here who have never had that born-again experience," Pastor continued. "Sometimes folks think they are saved just because they attend or were raised in church. Some think good behavior makes them Christians. Nothing could be further from the truth. You simply cannot earn salvation. If that were true, Jesus would not have died on the cross. He paid for our salvation with His blood. It's a gift. All of us were born in sin; therefore, we are sinners. We have to acknowledge that, and then confess that Jesus is Lord and believe in our hearts that God raised Him from the dead. When we do that, we will be saved. Anyone here like that? If you are, then please come forward now."

He laid his Bible on the pulpit and looked across the sanctuary. No one moved. He waited awhile before he and Thomas descended into the baptistry. When Thomas rose from the water, his hands were up, praising God. Lillian clasped her hands and looked back just in time to see Nathan grab Kora's hand and drag her down the aisle and out the door.

A weeping lady who had been a pillar of the church for years approached the front and spoke to Pastor Bill. "Pastor, I've claimed to be a Christian all this time. I thought coming to church and being a good person made me one, but you made me realize I have never been born again, as you say. I want that, Pastor. I want to experience what you're talking about."

They knelt together at the altar, and when they rose, Pastor Bill looked around to see the altar filled with people who were crying out to God in repentance. People lined up to confess their trust in Jesus before the weeping congregation.

<hr>

The next day, Lillian texted Kora. "Washington DC, November."

Kora replied. "Grand Canyon. Birthday party for 10-year-old."

Kora showed up at Lillian's house at ten the next day.

"What happened Sunday?" Lillian asked when she ushered Kora into the kitchen and poured her some tea.

"Nathan dragged me out and drove home like a maniac," she said. "He was livid. He kept swearing and accusing Pastor

Bill of manipulating Thomas and you into his 'web of deceit cult' as he put it. I tried to reason with him, but he wouldn't listen."

Lillian put her hand to her throat. "But I thought he claimed to be a Christian."

"He does. That's the kicker. To hear him talk, you'd think he doesn't even believe in church, or God for that matter. I gotta tell ya, I'm stumped. I don't know what to think anymore."

"Kora, don't be discouraged. We've been praying so hard, and we can't give up now. We know that things can get worse before they get better. Remember?"

Kora jumped up and paced around the room. She dragged her fingers through her hair and groaned. "How long, Lillian? I don't know how much more I can take. He's getting meaner and more demanding. Know what he did this morning? I fried some bacon and eggs for his breakfast, and he threw them at me. He said I was trying to poison him." She held up her arm. "See that red spot? That's a burn from the hot food."

"I'm so sorry, sweetie. Did you put something on it?"

"No. I just ran out of the house and stayed out of sight until he left for work."

Lillian went into the bathroom and returned with some burn medicine. When she pushed up Kora's sleeve to treat the wound, bruises and cuts were visible further up on her arm.

"What are these, Kora? Did Nathan do this to you?"

Kora nodded. "I told you he's getting meaner." She slumped in the chair, and tears coursed down her face. "I need some relief, Lillian. I don't know what to do. He says he'll kill me if I try to leave him." She straightened and looked up at Lillian. "Please don't tell Thomas, okay?"

Lillian treated the wounds and gently pulled down the sleeve. "No, I won't. But I know what to do. You're not going back home. You're going to stay here until we figure out something. I won't let him touch you, and now I'm sure Thomas will help us."

Kora's eyes widened, and she stood up. "I—I—I don't know, Lillian. What if he comes after me? He might hurt someone."

"No, he won't. Thomas will talk some sense into him. I'm sure of it. Thomas talked a long time last night about what he's been doing to me. He apologized so many times I had to ask him to stop. I explained that his wrongs are under the blood and gone forever. He kept thinking of the bad things he had done to me. He cried every time he thought of something else he did."

Kora gulped and wiped her eyes. "I want that for Nathan and me so bad. I long for him to love me again like he did when we first married. We were so happy then. I don't understand what happened. If I could understand, maybe I could fix it."

"No," said Lillian, "you can't fix what's wrong. It isn't your fault. Only God can help him come to his senses and make things right. You do understand that, right?"

"I guess. I know God can do anything we allow him to do."

"Then we'll keep praying for Nathan to listen to God and allow Him to do His work. Only that will change the situation. Give me your hands."

Lillian took Kora's hands and together, they prayed for Nathan.

About midnight, Lillian and Thomas awakened to a loud banging on the door. Thomas looked out the window. "It's Nathan," he said. "I kinda figured he'd show up here sooner or later."

He opened the door and stepped out onto the porch. "What's up, Nathan?"

"Is she here?" Nathan bellowed. "Is Kora here? I went to her folk's house, and they didn't know where she was. I figured she must be here."

"Just quiet down, man. You're waking up everyone." He reached for Nathan's arm to guide him off the porch, but Nathan jerked away.

"You just get her out here," he yelled. "Now."

"No," Thomas said. "I won't do that. You know why? Because she's scared of you. You've hurt her so much she can't take any more."

"She's my wife. I want her home where she belongs."

Thomas reached again for Nathan's arm, and this time Nathan allowed him to guide him off the porch. Lillian stood inside close enough to see and hear the two men from the window.

"Nathan, why did you marry Kora?"

Nathan frowned. "Why else would I marry her? I love her. I've always loved her."

"Do you think she loves you?" Thomas's voice was gentle.

"Uh, yeah, I guess so. At least she used to."

"Does she have any reason to stop loving you?"

"What are you trying to do, man? Ruin my marriage? What have you said to her? Are you trying to turn her against me?"

Thomas shook his head. "No, I don't want to turn her against you. I just want the two of you to work this thing out."

"Then get her out here, now!"

"No, I won't do that. It's her choice." He opened the door and looked inside. "Kora, do you want to come out and talk to Nathan?"

Kora responded in a small voice but loud enough for Nathan to hear. "No, not until he calms down. I won't come out."

Nathan slammed his fist against the porch post and whirled around. Lillian could see blood as he shook his hand and jumped into his vehicle. He spun his wheels as he drove off.

The next night, after Thomas and Lillian prepared for bed, Nathan beat on the door again. Kora, who had already retired to the guest room, ran into the living room and peered out.

"It's Nathan," she whispered. "Please tell him I don't want to talk to him. I can tell he's angry still."

"I'll talk to him." Thomas opened the door, and Nathan's fist almost hit Thomas in the face as he aimed another hard knock on the door.

"Get her out here, now!" Nathan yelled. "I want my wife. She belongs with me, not here."

Thomas closed the door behind him, and the two women stood close to the window, which was opened a crack.

"Nathan, you have to calm down. She's not going to talk to you as long as you're angry. And, obviously, you are very angry. Look at your tone and your expression. Anyone can tell you are fuming."

"Your blamed right, I'm mad. You'd be mad, too, if your wife was holed up at someone else's house."

"You're right, but we have to look at this from Kora's point of view. You might hide, too, if you thought someone was going to hurt you."

Nathan stared, frowning, his lips in a thin line. "She thinks I'm gonna hurt her?"

Thomas nodded slowly. "You've hurt her more than once, haven't you?"

Nathan whirled, jumped in his truck, and spun out.

The next two nights were quiet. Then he returned. This time, his knock was light, and his expression calm. "Come on, Thomas, open up. I'm ready to talk."

Thomas opened the door but refused to allow Nathan inside. "Let's talk out here on the porch."

They sat on the edge of the porch, and Nathan popped his knuckles and kept his eyes averted.

"Nathan, if you're ready to talk, maybe this thing can be resolved."

Nathan glanced at him and scuffed his boot on the ground. "Do you think she still loves me?"

"I don't know. Does she have reason not to love you?"

A long pause. "Uh, I don't think so. I guess not. Why?"

Thomas hesitated. "Please forgive me if I'm talking out of turn, but I care about you guys. You heard Pastor Bill say that I thought I was a Christian but found out I wasn't. That isn't all." He peered into Nathan's face. "Lillian left me, Nathan. It was a wake-up call for me. She gave it to me good, too. Told me I had been mistreating her. That I was mean to her, and she wasn't going to take it anymore. Said she never married me to be bullied."

Nathan gasped. "What? She accused you of bullying her?"

Thomas nodded. "And do you know what? She was right. I was bullying her. I was mistreating her. In fact, I was downright mean and hateful to her. Can you believe that?"

Nathan shook his head. "No, of course not. You couldn't do that. You're a nice guy."

Thomas chuckled. "I hope from now on I will be, but I haven't been. I've been a jerk. It took Lillian and God to make me see that. I had to change, and I'm glad."

"Really? I don't think I'm that bad. I think I'm a good husband."

"Then why is your wife sleeping at our house? What has it been like at your house the last couple of weeks? Huh?"

Nathan looked at the ground and walked a circle with his hands behind his back. He returned to stand beside Thomas. "We did have an argument before I left for work the day she left. It wasn't a big deal, though."

"I'm not trying to interfere in your life, but will you tell me what happened?"

"Uh, I didn't like the way she cooked my eggs for breakfast. I don't know what she did, but they didn't taste right. I threw them out, and it made her mad."

Thomas cocked his head. "You threw them out? Outside?"

"Well, no, not really. I just threw them." Nathan's face reddened, and he averted his eyes away from Thomas.

"So—you threw them in the floor?"

"In the floor, huh? You sure that's where you threw them? You know our ladies don't like their clean floors dirtied up."

"Yeah, she got really mad."

"Why did she get mad?"

"Because I threw the eggs on her—I mean, on the floor."

Thomas's eyes bugged out. "You threw hot eggs on her? What were you thinking?"

"Ah, they weren't that hot. I don't think so, anyway. But, Thomas, something was wrong with them. I think she's trying to poison me or something."

"Now, Nathan, you know that isn't likely. Is it possible that you imagined they tasted bad? Maybe you're just tired of eggs. Or maybe you were upset about something else."

"Well, maybe. I guess I have been a little cranky lately."

"Why have you been cranky? Is Kora doing something to make you cranky?"

"I don't know, Thomas. I don't know why I act the way I do. She's been telling me she's gonna leave me, but I didn't believe her."

He wiped his eyes. "I don't want my wife to leave me. What can I do?"

Thomas gestured for Nathan to sit on the porch swing and sat opposite him on a chair. He leaned forward and peered into Nathan's eyes.

"Nathan, she doesn't want to leave you, but you've left her no choice. She can't continue to live with a man who abuses her."

Nathan's head jerked up. "Abuses her? Did she say that?"

"Not to me, but I've seen the signs. I can recognize them because I abused Lillian until she left me."

"But—but she's with you now."

"You were at church Sunday, weren't you? I thought I saw you before service."

"Yes, I was there. I left early."

"Then you saw that I became a Christian," Thomas said.

"I'm already a Christian."

"Then why are you acting like a man who doesn't know God? A Christian man doesn't hit his wife, does he?"

"Uh, I guess not. But I go to church."

"Didn't you hear what Pastor Bill said? That lots of people think they're Christian because they go to church, but that doesn't make them Christian. Have you ever given your heart to Jesus? Have you made a confession of faith?"

Nathan frowned. "I don't know how to do that. Is that what you did?"

"Yes, Nathan. That's what I did. And it changed me. I feel different on the inside. I know I have a long way to go, but I'm starting to understand how to be a good husband and how to be a good man. What about you? Do you want to be changed on the inside?"

Nathan rubbed his head. "You really think I can change? I do want to be a good husband."

"Sure." Thomas put a hand on his shoulder. "If you sincerely want to change, then Jesus will change you. All you have to do is acknowledge that you are a sinner and ask Him into your heart. It's that simple."

"Will you help me?"

"I'm really new at this, but I can pray with you. If you want, we can go see Pastor Bill in the morning. He knows all about it and can help you better than I can."

"Yes, I want to do that. But I don't want to wait until morning. I'm afraid to wait."

"Well, that can be an issue. You probably need to go now so you won't be tempted to change your mind. I'll call Pastor. He says we can call him anytime we need him."

He went inside, and in a few minutes, Thomas, Lillian, Nathan, and Kora were sitting in Pastor Bill's office. Pastor Bill led Nathan to make a confession of faith, and they celebrated together.

The next Sunday, Nathan joined Pastor Bill in front of the congregation. "I want to confess before all of you," he said. "I have been needing the Lord for a long time now, but I kept pushing Him away. He wouldn't leave me alone, though, and I'm glad." He wiped his eyes and spoke between sobs. "I want to make a public apology to my wife. I have not honored the vows I made to her when we married. I've been mean and hateful to her. She's been sweet and forgiving, and she doesn't deserve the treatment I've given her."

Tears streaming down her face, Kora threw her arms around him. Thomas and Lillian went to them, and they all cried together. Pastor Bill asked Nathan if he wanted to be baptized, and he nodded. His face glowed, and his eyes glistened.

Before he dismissed the service, Pastor Bill confessed to everyone. "Recently, I had some members of this church come to me with a problem, and I didn't believe them. I am so sorry I did that. I don't deserve to be your Pastor if I don't listen to you and trust you." He pulled out a handkerchief and blew his nose. A murmur rose from the congregation as he bowed his head.

A man spoke up from the middle of the crowd. "We forgive you, Pastor Bill."

Another voice rose, this time a woman. "You're only

human, Pastor. We all make mistakes." Then another. "We love you, Pastor Bill." "Yes, yes," came from all over the building. Finally, Pastor Bill dismissed, and the people lingered, not wanting to leave with such a sweet spirit hovering over them. Pastor talked privately to Nathan and Kora about the counseling program, and they agreed to attend.

As they were leaving, Lillian and Kora held back. "Thank you, Pastor," they said.

He squeezed their hands. "Ladies, I apologize. I am so sorry I ignored your pleas for help."

"We accept your apology," Lillian said. Kora smiled at him.

"What about Bella?" he asked. "I haven't seen her for a while."

"She said this week she would tell Levi to leave," Kora said. "We haven't seen her since last Wednesday."

"Oh." He passed his hand over his face. "I will blame myself if anything happens to her."

Lillian shook her head. "Levi hit Trevor. That did it for her. She won't stand for her kids to be in danger. Do you think you could talk to him?"

Pastor nodded. "Yes, I will do that right away. Do you know where he is?" The two women shook their heads. "Then I'll drive out that way. Maybe Bella will know."

THIRTY-NINE

*B*ella didn't have the heart to attend church since the meeting with Pastor Bill. Her eyes sparked, and her fists clenched when she thought about his words. How could he not believe them? He wouldn't even listen. He was her pastor, for heaven's sake! He was the pastor of the women as well at the men. At least, he was supposed to be.

She loaded sheets into the dryer and turned it on, then dumped shirts and detergent into the washing machine. Addie and Trevor had cleaned the kitchen after lunch and were watching television. The day she hoped would be a day of rest turned out to be a stressful housework day.

A knock at the door sounded. "Trevor, will you see who's out there?" she yelled.

"It's Dad," Trevor answered. "I'm not opening the door." He headed for his bedroom.

"Me either," Addie said. She also left the room.

"Now, what in the world does he want?" Bella looked out, then jerked the door open. Levi stood there holding out a bouquet of roses.

"What do you want?"

"Bella, please forgive me. I've been such a jerk. Please let me come home."

"Go away, Levi. We don't want you here."

"Please, Bella. I've changed. I won't be mean to you anymore. I've quit drinking. I'll get a job, I promise."

She stared at him, then shook her head. "I don't believe you. You'd say anything and promise anything to move back into this house. Well, it's not happening."

"Aww, come on, Bella. You know I love you. I miss you and the kids."

"You want to move back in to beat on us again? No way. Just go back to the hole you've been staying in."

He threw the bouquet on the porch and turned to leave. She shouted after him. "I'm filing for a divorce in case you're interested."

He turned and raised one finger to her. She rolled her eyes, slammed the door behind her, and hissed. He's nothing but a snake in the grass trying to slither his way back. Wait! A prick in her mind stopped her. Snake? She recalled the entry in her journal about a snake. She stomped her foot. "I will not quit!" she declared. "The man just at my door is not my husband. My husband is sweet and loves me. I will not give up on him. I am strong. God is my fortress, and I will trust Him."

She straightened her shoulders and lifted her head as she pulled towels from the dryer and folded them. She had just sat down to watch TV with the kids when another knock sounded. "That had better not be your dad again," she said.

Addie looked out the window. "Nope. It's Pastor Bill."

Bella groaned. "Oh, no, not him." She went to the door. "Hello, Pastor Bill."

"Good to see you, Bella," he said. "You've been missing some good services."

"Well, I've been busy. Sorry I've been missing."

"May I come in? I need to talk to you."

She moved to one side and opened the door wider so he could enter. "Please, have a seat. Addie, bring a glass of tea for the pastor."

He adjusted his tie and sat where she indicated. "Bella, I owe you a huge apology," he said. "I'm so sorry I did not listen to you ladies when you came to me with your problem. Will you please forgive me?"

She stared at him. "Really? What made you change your mind?"

"Thomas. Thomas Thorn. And Nathan Sharp. Do you know them?"

"Sure," Bella said. "He's Lillian's husband. And Nathan is Kora's husband. I know them both."

"Yes, of course. Have you heard they've both been baptized?"

"Now, how could I hear that? I haven't been anywhere or seen anyone from church, at least. So how did that change your mind?"

"They both confessed to mistreating their wives. Bella, I'm so sorry I didn't believe you ladies. I know now that you were asking for help, and I didn't listen to you."

Bella lowered her head. "I'm glad for Lillian and Kora. But that doesn't help me. Levi is still mean, still drinking, and still jobless. I'm no better off. Does that mean God loves me less?"

"Oh, no! Of course not! Sometimes, it takes Him a little longer to bring some people around. I'm sure He's working on Levi, but Levi doesn't want to listen. He may need to be sober long enough to hear God speaking to him."

Bella scoffed. "Well, I don't know how that's gonna happen. He stays drunk most of the time. He came to the door a little while ago with flowers, begging to move back in. I'll betcha he was at least partly drunk then. By now, he's soused."

"Do you know where I can find him? I'd like to try to talk to him."

"I'm not sure, but I believe he's staying at his mom's house. Do you know where she lives?"

"Yes, I know her. I'll go there to see if I can find him."

After he left, Bella picked up her journal and wrote.

Dear Journal: It's me again. Still down and out. I don't think God loves me. Thomas and Nathan have changed—good for Lillian and Kora. But Levi has only gotten worse. I don't know what to do. I guess I'll see a lawyer and file for a divorce. I don't want to, but I can't keep on living like this. If only he'd change like he says he has. But I know he hasn't. He just wants to come home, so he'll have a place to live and someone to beat on. If he ever hurts one of my kids again, I may kill him. I only wish God would do it so I wouldn't have to. I don't want to go to prison for murder. Then, my kids wouldn't have a mom or a dad.

I've prayed and prayed—even fasted—and nothing good has happened for me. Why does my husband have to be so hardheaded and mean? I don't deserve it. I deserve a husband who loves me and the kids. I remember reading in the Bible that a husband is to love his wife as much as he loves himself. And like Christ loves the church. Levi wouldn't do to himself what he does to me. And Christ gave himself for the church. Levi won't even give me the time of day.

We used to be so in love. We were so happy. What happened? Then he started looking at porn and drinking. Next thing, he had another woman. Then, he became a soddy drunk. I've tried to talk to him, but it does no good. Pastor says God is talking to him, but he won't listen. What am I to do? Don't I deserve a better life than this?

Lord, if you love me at all, I'm asking that you don't give up on him or me. We need you more than ever. My kids need you. They need a dad who cares about them and their mom so they will learn how to care about others. Amen

FORTY

*L*illian was surprised when Thomas wanted to go watch a movie on Saturday night. That's one thing he never wanted to do after they were married. When they arrived at the cinema, they met Brian and April Robbins from church.

"How nice to see you here," Brian said. "I didn't think you guys ever went to the movies.

Thomas laughed. "We never used to, but I thought it'd make a nice treat. And since it's a Christian movie, it should be good."

They loaded up with popcorn and sodas and sat together in the theater. Thomas chatted with Brian, and Lillian enjoyed talking with April. After the movie, Thomas suggested they get some ice cream. Lillian learned that she and April enjoyed many of the same things, and when April invited Lillian over for a visit, Thomas encouraged her to accept. On the way home, Lillian mentioned that her daughter Eva's birthday fell on Tuesday of the following week.

"Why don't you give her a birthday party?" Thomas asked. "We can have it at the house. Your kids can bring their families, and we can have a cookout. I'll smoke a brisket, and you can make some of your delicious sides. It'll be fun." For the first time, Lillian could invite her family to her house. It made her so happy to see a real clue that he truly had changed.

One day, she met Fran, a woman who worked in the

courthouse down the hall from Thomas. She'd met her a few times but didn't know her well.

"Thomas sure has changed," Fran said. "What happened to him? He used to be so—uh—so arrogant, but lately, he seems nice. Different. He actually smiles and talks to those of us who work in the offices."

Lillian smiled. "He got his life right with God," she said.

"Really?" Fran raised her eyebrows. "How did that happen?"

"He went to see Pastor Bill at church, and Pastor Bill led him to the Lord."

"Going to church changed him that much?"

"Oh, going to church didn't. He's been going to church a long time. He's had a heart change. He repented and gave his heart to the Lord. That changed him."

Fran pulled on her collar and bit her lip. "I don't understand. What do you mean, gave his heart to the Lord?"

Lillian explained the plan of salvation and how it changes people who believe. She answered Fran's questions. She was amazed that Fran seemed completely ignorant about Jesus and how He shed His blood to redeem mankind. At the end of the conversation, Fran agreed to visit church with Lillian to learn more.

Back at home, Thomas threw the duty list he'd made for her early in the marriage into the trash. He encouraged her to cook whatever she wanted for his meals. "I'll enjoy trying some new recipes," he said. "When you go grocery shopping, you can pick up the ingredients to make some things you've been wanting to try." His facial expressions were different. She loved that he flashed those sexy dimples much more often. He treated her with such gentleness and tenderness and complimented everything she did. She had witnessed the power of God change people before, and it never ceased to amaze her when it happened so quickly. For the zillionth time in the last few days, she offered a silent thanks to God.

At the *lieu de rencontre* the following week, Lillian and Kora tried to contain their joy to benefit Bella, who hardly spoke when she first arrived.

"Pastor Bill visited me and told me what happened at church with your husbands," she said. She tried to smile, but only one side curled up. "I'm truly glad for y'all. Maybe one day it will happen to me."

"We're believing that it will," said Lillian. "Bella, we won't stop praying and believing for Levi. Pastor Bill has the whole church praying. Maybe Levi won't hold out much longer."

"Is there anything we can do?" asked Kora. "Any way we can help? We know you have a heavy load to bear. Are the kids okay?"

Bella nodded. "The kids are fine. And I'm fine. Levi came over the other day with a bunch of roses, asking me to let him come home. Says he's changed, but I don't believe him. Pastor Bill says he would try to find him and talk to him. I don't know if he did."

"Kora and I will continue to fast and pray," Lillian said, "until Levi changes by giving his heart to Christ. Right, Kora?"

"You'd better believe it."

"I appreciate y'all so much," Bella said. "I couldn't do this without your help. I am trying to speak more positively, and I'm praying for him all the time that he'll listen to God."

"We're with you, dear," Lillian said. "We won't give up."

"Say," Kora said. "Remember that woman at church who is always sad? I found out who she is."

"Who is she?" asked Lillian. "And how did you find out?"

"Sunday after church, Nathan pointed her out to me. Her name is Marcy. Her husband is Mikie."

"What?" Bella said. "Marcy is married to Mikie?"

Kora nodded. "That's her. Nathan said he hadn't noticed her before, but that's who she is. No wonder she's sad all the time. "I'll bet it's the same Mikie from the letter."

Lillian blinked. "Now I remember. I thought that handwriting looked familiar. Marcy is the one who sends cards to people who miss church, and she sent one to Thomas and me when we missed once. Wow! I can't imagine her threatening to kill someone, can you? I mean, she didn't say she'd kill them, but it sure sounded like that."

"I sure can't," said Kora. "She always seems so quiet and gentle. Guess you never know what's going on inside a person."

"Wow! I've been praying for her ever since I talked to her at the church dinner." Lillian's eyes gleamed. "Wow! God works in mysterious ways. Now we know what she's going through, we can pray for her specifically. Ladies, that means we have to double up on our prayers for her."

"I'll say," said Kora. "We know what prayers can do."

Lillian grasped Bella's hands. "And Bella, we're believing for a miracle to happen for you, and soon."

Bella nodded, and they prayed together before they went home.

FORTY-ONE

*E*arly on Saturday morning, a knock sounded on the door while Bella mopped the kitchen. "Hello, Pastor Bill. What brings you by on such a beautiful day?"

Pastor Bill rubbed the back of his neck. "I went to see Levi's parents, and he isn't there. His dad says they kicked him out when he came home drunk the first night." He glanced away then back at her. "Bella, Levi's in jail."

Bella gasped. "In jail? What did he do?"

"The officer found him drunk and disorderly, so he locked him up to get him off the street. He said when he sobers up, you can pick him up. That is, if you want to."

"Do I have to?"

"No. I can go get him if you don't want to, but then I don't know where he'll go."

Bella pushed her hair back and groaned. "Looks like I'll have to. I can't have him living on the streets."

Pastor drove Bella to the police station, and an officer brought Levi out. His eyes were bloodshot, and his face unshaven. His clothes were dirty and disheveled. He smelled of alcohol and bad body odor. He kept his eyes on the floor and shuffled his feet.

"I'm sorry, Bella," he mumbled. She nodded and pushed

him toward the door. As they approached Pastor Bill's SUV, he stumbled, and Bella grabbed his arm and guided him into the back seat.

When Pastor Bill pulled into Bella's drive, Levi sat still, watching Bella. She opened the back door and gestured for him to get out.

"Are you gonna let me stay here?" he said.

"Depends."

"Oh." He slid out of the seat and looked at her.

"Thank you, Pastor Bill," she said. "I can handle it from here."

He looked from her to Levi. "Are you sure? I can take him to the mission if you want."

"No. It's okay. He can stay as long as he behaves."

She waved as Pastor Bill drove away, and then she went into the house, leaving Levi standing on the porch.

When he finally shuffled through the door, she looked him up and down. "The first thing you can do is shower. You smell like a pig. I have to go to the store to buy some groceries. When I get back, we'll talk."

"Okay. I'm sorry, Bella."

She sniffed. "Just clean up. I'll be back after while."

When Bella returned home, she found Levi sitting on the couch holding her journal. "What in the world are you doing?" she yelled. "How dare you get into my personal things."

He looked up at her. Tears were running down his face, and his hands trembled. "Is this how you feel?" he asked. "You feel like God doesn't love you because of me? You want God to kill me?"

Bella shifted from one foot to the other. "Well, I..."

"Have I really changed so much? Am I this bad?" His face contorted, and he looked back at the journal. "Oh, Bella, I'm sorry. I have been wrong. I have treated you and the kids so wrong." He stood and walked toward her. "You do deserve a husband who'll treat you right. What happened to the love we used to share?"

She shook her head. "I don't know, Levi. I just don't know."

He sobbed. "I do. I know what happened. I lost my way. I made bad decisions. It's all my fault. Can you ever forgive me?"

He sat down on the couch, and she sat beside him. She spoke in a whisper. "Levi, I forgive you. Over and over, I forgive you. But you have to make a permanent change. I mean, you have to change on the inside."

"How do I do that?" He clenched his fists. "I'll quit drinking. I'll be good to you and the kids. I promise."

She took his dirty hands in hers. "Your promises aren't enough, sweetheart. You'll end up right back doing the same things. You need to repent to God. He's the only One who can change you on the inside." She leaned over and peered into his face. "And He can do that."

"Really? Do you think He will? I mean, do you think He'll change me? Cause I don't think I can do it myself."

"If you'll ask Him, I know He'll forgive you and change you."

He stared at her. "I don't know how. What if He won't forgive me? I've done terrible things, and I don't deserve anything from God."

"Pastor Bill says none of us deserve anything from God, no matter how good or bad we are. He says Jesus died so everyone could come to God no matter who or what we are. Just ask Him, Levi. Try." She pulled his arm, guiding him to his knees beside the couch, and knelt beside him.

As he cried out to God for forgiveness, she cried with him. When they finally rose, she hugged him. "We need to go see Pastor Bill," she said. "He can help you understand what God will do to change you." He agreed.

While he showered and changed, Bella called to make an appointment with the Pastor. Pastor Bill met them at the church door with open arms. Thrilled when they told him the news, he laughed and hugged them both. "Looks like we're in for another baptismal service," he said.

"Pastor Bill...." Levi faltered. "I don't know if I can change. I want to, but what if I can't?"

Pastor Bill patted his shoulder. "Son, you can't change. But God can change you. He works on the inside, changing the heart. When you confess Jesus as your Savior, Jesus moves right inside you, and you'll see changes start happening. Can you believe that?"

Levi's brows furrowed. "That doesn't sound possible, sir."

Pastor laughed. "That's where faith comes in. First, you must recognize that you were born a sinner in need of salvation. Then, you accept Jesus by faith. Do you believe in Jesus?"

Levi nodded.

"Do you believe Jesus died for your sins and that God raised Him from the dead?"

"I haven't thought much about it, but yeah, I guess I do. I've always heard about Him doing that. But I never took it serious."

"Then you're on the right road that leads to salvation. The Bible says if you believe in your heart and confess with your mouth the Lord Jesus, you will be saved."

Levi's eyes widened. "That's all I have to do? And that will change me? I know I can't change myself."

"That's right, son. That's what you have to do. Jesus paid the price, so you don't have to do anything but believe and confess."

"All right, then." Levi lifted a hand. "I believe Jesus died for me. I believe God raised Him from the dead." He looked up. "Jesus, I am a sinner, and I need You. I'm sorry for my sins. Will you come in and change me? I sure do need changed, and Pastor says you can do it. I'll sure appreciate it if you'll do that for me."

Bella stood beside him, smiling. Pastor Bill grabbed his

hand and shook it hard. "Son," he said, "I'm so proud and thankful you've found the Lord."

Levi grinned. "I think it's more likely He found me. And I sure am glad." He turned to Bella. "Sweetheart, I sure am sorry for the way I've treated you. With the help of Jesus, I'll be good to you from now on."

She hugged him, beaming. "I know you will." She turned to Pastor Bill. "Thank you, Pastor, for everything."

"No, not me. Jesus is the one who has done this. He works miracles all the time, you know." He turned to Levi. "He is faithful, and he heard your cry for help."

Levi stood, smiling at Bella and Pastor. "Now what?"

Pastor put his hand on his shoulder. "Son, I'm not going to tell you it will be easy. Usually nothing is. But I will tell you that God will be with you, helping you when you ask Him and let Him. Just be aware of His constant presence by reading His word and talking to Him. Should you be tempted to fall back into old habits, ask Him to help you, and He will. Also, I advise you to join an AA group. I can hook you up with one. They will help you physically and spiritually."

"That's good to know, sir. I'm sure Bella will help me. I sure don't want to go back to my old life. I already feel different."

Pastor Bill gripped his hand. "She will help you, and I know she'll always pray for you. That's the most important thing." He put his hand on their shoulders. "There is one more thing you both need to consider. Marriage counseling. I know a Christian husband and wife team who can help you with issues that may come up in the future."

Levi and Bella agreed. When they returned home, Levi helped Bella prepare supper and clean up after. "You know," he said, "I've never thought about it before now, but you've had to do everything around here by yourself. I could have been helping you all this time. From now on, I will do my share. And when I get back to work, soon you'll be able to cut your hours back to a couple of days a week if you want."

She pushed her hair behind her ears. "We will decide that later," she said. "With you helping me around the house, I won't have so much to do. Of course, you may want me here to tend to the cattle while you're at work. We'll figure it out."

She put her arms around his neck. "I love you so much. I'm glad to get reacquainted with the husband I first married."

He grinned and embraced her. "Oh, I intend to be even better than the old Levi in every way." He pulled her to his chest and kissed her.

Trevor barreled through the door with Addie close behind. They stopped short when they saw their parents. "Mom! Dad!" Trevor covered his face. "Please!"

"Not in the kitchen," Addie said. "How embarrassing."

"What the matter, kids?" Levi laughed. "Haven't you ever seen grown-up kissing?"

"Well, not in a while." Trevor grabbed a cookie from the counter. "At least, not you two."

"Yeah," Addie said, "But it's really nice. Go ahead, we'll leave."

They both laughed and ran into the living room. Soon, the TV blared, and Bella returned to Levi's embrace.

FORTY-TWO

*L*illian picked up a shopping basket and headed down the aisle at the Dollar General. Loving the freedom she now had to shop and have friends, she, Bella, and Kora often went shopping together.

"Here's a cute lamp," Kora said. "Wouldn't it look good in my bathroom? I've been wanting a little one to use as a nightlight."

Bella picked up another one. "This one is cute, too," she said. "I need it to replace the one I broke when I crawled through the window."

"Did you ever hide an extra key somewhere outside in case you lock yourself out again?" asked Kora.

"I sure did. I glued a rock on the lid of a medicine container and put a key in it. I hid it in my flower bed. Now I should never have to crawl through another window."

Hearing Lillian speak to someone, they both turned and recognized Marcy from church.

"You ladies out enjoying a day of shopping?" Marcy smiled and started to move on when Lillian stopped her.

"Are you doing okay, Marcy?" Lillian asked. "I've been a little concerned about you. I think God has put you on my heart for some reason, so I've been praying for you."

Marcy blinked. "Yeah, I'm okay, I guess. Thanks for thinking of me. I sure can use as many prayers as I can get."

Lillian lowered her voice. "Would you like to talk about — things?"

Marcy looked at each of the women facing her. "I am happy about what happened at church with your husbands. That's wonderful. I sure could use some of that." She lowered her head. "I would like to talk to you ladies. I've talked to Pastor Bill some, but it would be nice to talk to someone who understands what I'm going through."

Lillian put the items in the basket back on the shelves. Kora and Bella did the same. Then, they led Marcy out of the store.

"We need somewhere private," Lillian said. She led them to the new SUV Thomas had purchased for her. They crawled into the vehicle and waited for Marcy.

"It seems like a quick, simple thing that happened with our men," Lillian said. "I guess in comparison to some situations, it happened pretty quick, but it wasn't simple."

"How — how long has the trouble been going on," asked Marcy.

"Not as long for me," Lillian said. "Thomas and I have been married a while now, but the abuse started almost immediately after we married."

"Nathan and I have been married for two years," said Kora, "but the abuse started about a year ago."

Bella drew in a deep breath. "Levi wasn't abusive for most of our marriage. He was a stinker with his cursing and bellowing, but only in the last couple of years did he start being abusive. That started with his increasing drinking habit. And then, he had an affair. He was worse after that."

"Mikie really isn't abusive," Marcy said. "Actually, I don't think he cares about me at all. Most of the time, I don't think he knows I exist. He's so busy chasing other women. That has been his habit for years. He's had three affairs, and this last one has been going on for over a year. I'm tired of it."

"We've been praying for you," Bella said.

"How did you know?" Marcy's eyes were wide. "I didn't think anyone even guessed."

Kora told her about the letter in the woods, and they explained how it all came together when they learned who Mikie was and who she was.

Marcy sighed. "I wondered what he did with that. He never would listen when I tried to get him to talk about things. I should have known he would never even read something I wrote." Suddenly, her eyes widened. "I think I may have made a threat in that letter. Of course, I would never do something like that. I wanted to shake him up. I guess it didn't work."

"He probably didn't even read the whole thing," Lillian said. "Looks like he wadded it up and threw it out the window when he drove down the road."

"We will continue to pray for healing for your marriage," Bella said. "It sure did make a difference in ours."

Marcy shook her head. "It's over. He has no intentions of changing. I did mean what I said, that if he wouldn't agree to start over, I was done."

"But God can change him," Kora said. "Look what He did for us."

"Not if he refuses to change," Marcy said. "God won't force him. I've spent years praying for him and waiting for him to change."

"It's true that a person must want to change." Lillian took Marcy's hand. "No one can or will force him. But we can still pray for him. Would you like to talk to Pastor Bill again?"

"I can, but I tell you it won't do any good. Like I said, I've been praying and believing for the man to change for years."

Lillian started the vehicle, and they drove to see Pastor Bill. He listened to the situation and then suggested they pray. The women held hands while he prayed for Marcy and Mikie.

"Want me to talk to him?" Pastor Bill asked. Marcy agreed as long as she wasn't present for the conversation.

On Friday, Marcy requested a meeting with Pastor Bill and asked Lillian, Kora, and Bella to go with her.

"Pastor Bill, since you've talked to Mikie, he is so hateful and mean to me," she said. "He said I sicced you on to him, and he doesn't want anything to do with church or those so-called Christians. I'm filing for a divorce next week. He's ruined our finances, and I can't take anymore. I won't take anymore."

Pastor Bill bowed his head. "I understand," he said. "We ask God to do a lot of things, and we trust Him." He looked back up at the sad faces before him. "But you're right. He won't force anyone to change. Marcy, I know you've prayed for that man a long time. You have every reason to leave him. Every marriage can't be saved. I hate it, but no one blames you."

Marcy wiped her eyes and hugged her three friends.

"Please call us if you need a shoulder," Lillian said.

"Or if you want friends to go shopping with," Kora added.

"Or if you just need a good laugh," Bella said. "We can help with that."

"Thank you, ladies and Pastor." Marcy smiled. "I'm glad God gave me some new friends."

FORTY-THREE

On Sunday, Pastor Bill stood before the congregation, tearful and smiling. "Well," he said, "hell has lost another one." He gazed across the congregation of people who looked at each other, confused. He held out his hand. "Stand up, Levi. Let these people see a changed man. Folks, the devil couldn't keep this soul any longer. He has surrendered his life to Jesus."

Loud applause sounded throughout the building as Levi walked to the baptistry. Pastor Bill explained that he would baptize Levi and preach his sermon afterward. When Levi rose from the water, the praise team sang, "Hallelujah, all my sins are washed away!" and the audience cheered.

Pastor Bill stood behind the pulpit, barefooted and wet. He looked over the people for a moment before he began.

"Folks," he said, "I have been preaching a long time and have never addressed the topic I will present today. It isn't that the problem didn't exist or that it wasn't important. But it seems like an issue so many of us ministers avoid. I don't know why, except it is a tedious subject and can be embarrassing to address. But this issue has risen almost to epidemic proportions in today's world, even in the church."

He hesitated and adjusted his tie. "Husbands, how have you been treating your wives? Wives, how are you treating your husbands?" He paused and gazed over his audience.

"The church has become an ideal place to hide your marriage problems. You can give your offerings, sing the songs, and amen the preacher. Some of you men put your arms around your wife as you both listen to the sermon, and it's the same arm that you use to hurt her when you're in the home you've built together. The same voice used to sing praises to God is used to berate the spouse sitting beside you. You smile at your pew mates and pretend everything is fine. But if your spouse would tell the truth, you're far from fine. In fact, you're broken.

"How long has it been since you've shown love to your spouse? Instead, some of you sit in front of your TV or on the internet watching pornography or other vile programs that depict violence, vulgar language, and sexual scenes. You engage in or dream of unmentionable acts with people like those you've been watching, forgetting your wife at home. Then, you expect her to accept your attention with wide open arms. Some of you men treat your wives worse than you would treat a stranger or even an enemy. If you look closely at your neighbor, you might see black eyes and bruises under all that makeup or wounded spirits under those big smiles.

"And you women. I'm not ignoring your bad behaviors. Some of you spend more time nagging and griping at your husbands than you do loving and supporting them."

The congregation sat quietly, with a slight rustling as some shifted in their seats. Most eyes stared toward the front, but some eyes were downcast. Some men put their arms around the shoulders of their wives, and many wives folded their arms around themselves.

"Men, do you know," Pastor continued, "that your prayers won't be answered when you fail to honor and show consideration to your wife? In Paul's letter to the Ephesians, he says husbands are to love their wives as Christ loved the church. Can you imagine Jesus treating the church like you treat your wives? Wives, are you more of a hindrance to your husband's Christian walk than a help? Do you cause him so much stress he regrets he married you? Do you give him headaches or bring him happiness? Can you imagine Jesus treating your husband like you treat him?

"Folks, how do you think your spouse prays for you? Is it a prayer of thanksgiving for your love and kindness, or is it a request for relief from the pain you cause?

"The greatest thing you can do to help — in fact, to save — your marriage is to read God's word and pray together. But that won't accomplish anything if you continue to treat each other with disrespect. God wants to bless you through your spouse. When you bless your spouse, your spouse can bless others. Your children, family members, friends, and many others are affected when you work together and honor the Lord. When you dishonor one another, the effect is just as great, but it is a negative effect. Your children learn by watching you. How can you expect them to act right when you don't? How can you expect your children to learn how to properly treat a spouse by watching you mistreat yours? Other people see that you profess to serve and honor God while you act like you don't even know Him. You, as a follower of Jesus Christ, are to imitate Him. He gave us examples of love and compassion for everyone, and that includes your spouse."

He paused and walked to one side of the podium. He stood with one hand on his Bible, gazing over the quiet congregation. Then he gestured toward the altar. "If any of you want to start making things right in your home and your marriage, this altar is open. Men, as the head of the home, I invite you to make a stand. Take your wife by the hand and lead her toward a better marriage and a better life. Ladies, show your willingness to move toward a better life with your husband. I won't beg or twist your arms. The choice is yours."

All over the building, men held out hands to tearful wives, and together, they moved to the front to kneel. Thomas, Nathan, and Levi, leading their wives, were the first to reach the altar. A younger couple with a cute, freckled faced little boy kneeled together. The little boy squeezed between them, and they put their arms around him. In the back, Marcy wiped her eyes and blew her nose. She could rejoice with her new friends even if her Mikie refused to make a change. Maybe someday, he would see the truth and change. In the meantime, she could move on with her life. At least now she had friends who would encourage her and pray for her. She smiled. God was faithful. He'd heard and answered her prayers, even though not in the way she thought and hoped. His love and His presence surrounded her. She would be all right.